Telling of Contents

A Brief History of Kings - Book One

KINGS OF ANGELON

Foreword

I endeavored to write a more complete history of these lands, beginning with the Tasking of Tiluma in the ancient Realm of Margon and stretching all the way forth into this present year, 5573. I have not yet proven up to that task. However I have completed what could be described as a complete history of sorts on one period in particular, for it is where I began my writing, being most acquainted with these legends and tales. They are stories from the ancient Kingdom of Angelon, kingdom of 500 years, that which followed the early civilization of Therok and was followed by the Ilandian Empire.

In total, fourteen Kings* lorded over the land we speak of: they were Francil, Penflath, Grand Marc Vicar, Naegeli, Raedym, Wilderfrant (of which there were eight, and in some ways nine, in sequence), and DANE. This account spells over their reigns, with some in greater detail than others, and also deals with the more ancient times that transpired in the ages before their coming. For those who wish to read in an order of chronology, with the foundations of all Elaptirius set before the foundations of Angelon, then swiftly proceed to Part Three, which deals with Gods and Starlings and lords of ancient places.

For those who wisely opt to begin where I myself began, proceed forward without leaps, and you will find a brief history of the Nephinarthins of the Third and Fourth Ages, leading into the rise of Therok.

— Miryid Ilia

*Do be assured that the word King, in my country at least, is used to refer to both werman and woman rulers. The non-ruling spouse of a King is then called either Queen or Quoren, those words being based upon gender. As a brief starting fact, allow me to say that there were 99 werman kings and 23 woman kings in the combined span of Therok, Angelon, and Ilandia, making for 122 Kings in total. We are now in the midst of their 123rd ruler, but neither I nor he count himself amidst the others, for he has expanded the width of Ilandia to include all of Eastern Elaptirius, something I find to be rather alarming.

A Brief History of the Ancient Nephinarthins

The first civilized peoples settled along the Sea in what we now refer to as the Third Age. These Passian Men settled along the great inland water which they called Cathuma, and created the first permanent settlements of which we have any record. Perhaps their most famous deed was the establishment of a method that revealed the course of time— one day a child dropped a stick into a pit. The next day, she dropped another. And all those around her shrugged off the incident, thinking nothing of the stupid little girl who kept dropping sticks into pits. But eventually this stick-dropping was revealed as a way to track the comings and goings of day and night, and of the seasons and the passing of winds.

So the Nephinarthins put the tossing of the sticks into the hands of their great fingered chieftain, and from that day on, any other who tossed a stick into the Grand Pit were either castrated or plugged with fish. To the Nephinarthins then, the first Twig Tossing marked the beginning of what they would call the First Year. After a hundred years had passed, the Nephinarthins realized that more hundreds of years might come to pass, and so they recalibrated their dates, and said that the First Year was now the Hundredth Year. In this way, they could refer to the first century as the period from 100 to 199, and the second century as 200 to 299, and so on. We reckon now to be in the year 5573 based on the keeping of time that first began with the Twig Tossing of the Nephinarthins.

After a few hundred years of solitude, the Nephinarthins who lived on the curved eastern shore of Cathuma begin to trade— and trade fairly at that— with their neighbors to the north and south, as well as understand one another although they all began in different tongues. They did not war with each other, which is something quite remarkable for this period. Perhaps they realized it was their common interest to put all their efforts towards the shore, for great raiders would sail in from the far West Shores of Parpishaly on a near daily basis and run up the beaches with blade.

The Nephinarthins were a curious lot; despite being constantly harassed by the sailors of the sea, they refused to move. Their home was their home, and going anywhere else seemed to them the greatest farce. They loved to waddle here and there down the beaches, but always they returned. Even when they meant not to.

For a small group of Nephinarthins eventually set out in a westerly direction, holding steady to their beloved sea and never stepping off the sands. They did not stop; with tired legs they forged on, thinking true that one day they would come to a point where they could walk no further on, and gaze upon the ends of Cotialla— that is, all that exists.

But to their surprise, when they finally did come to Journey's End, they saw that they had ended exactly where they had started.

We begin The Fourth Age, it is supposed, in roughly the year 900, with the new-found knowledge of the Nephinarthins that the Sea of Cathuma is— in fact— not all that large, and can be walked around on foot within the span of a few weeks. This led to increased travel, and consequently increased communication with the folk over in Parpishaly who had been slicing, stealing, and snaking up the legs of the Nephinarthins for generations.

With the sharing of pivotal knowledge, the Passian peoples of Nephinarthos thus began to sail themselves, and with their boats, they made the Sea to be truly their own. An advanced system of writing and record-keeping also evolved at this time, but the Sea Dwellers would much rather leave us with the picture of them in their boats, possibly cutting out their teeth at sunrise to placate the wrath of the Glorious Sea Cunt— an apparently all-powerful goddess who would have been lost to time were it not for a wall in the Ligian Cave. Although, as we shall come to find, the Ligian Cave is the work of a later conquering force, and therefore the Glorious Sea Cunt and the sacrificial teeth may just be a later fabrication, as such things do not appear anywhere in Classical Nephinarthin tablets.

What does appear in Classical Nephinarthin tablets is as follows:

They shared toilets. As many as ten folk might use one single toilet— that is, a round seat with a hole in the middle for defecations to then fall into the earth. Still to this day do most men share toilets, for there are simply not enough toilets in existence for every man to have his or her own in their position; this in itself is nothing strange. What one might find strange, however, is that the Nephinarthins would share toilets at the same time as one another. It was in fact law that no man defecate without the company of another seated upon the same toilet. And when I say that up to ten men at a time might share the same toilet, I do mean that all ten would make use of it on the same set of moments.

The Nephinarthins, then, were not shy of each other's asses. In truth, it is said that their greatest ecstasy was achieved in the following manner: in the middle of long starlit nights, folk would sit upon the sands within earshot of crashing waves, and a Ceremonial Joybringer would walk around to every circle of friends, holding out an object of any kind. The friends in the circle would inquire as to what it was that the Joybringer held. And always "this is your ass" would the Joybringer say. This, then, is how the Nephinarthins preferred to pass their nights.

The hysterics of the Joybringing were reserved though, for special occasion, to be achieved only through the effective use of a Flip Nibbler. Otherwise the whole affair simply wasn't humorous, at all. Flip Nibblers were seaborne creatures, a cross between fish and snake, and nibble on the flips of wermen they did. Everything concerning this creature had to be precise— if the temperature or the positioning of the Flip Nibblers were awry, then maximum pleasure could not be obtained by the Joybringings. And as the Flip Nibblers would only arrive in the shallows of Cathuma every autumn, then for the rest of the year the Joybringings were but an eager anticipation for the wermen of the Sea.

The women of the sea sought pleasure in a more obtainable means. Every night, when the first sun in the South had shone its last, they would dress themselves in massive furs, and begin speaking to one another in the tongues of the beast. When the second sun dropped in the West, then they would rise up, and begin to dance. If any werman approached at this time, whether it be a fool or a priest, he would be torn into by severed fang all the same.

Therefore, the wermen approached not the women in the time of starlit hours, and because of this, they would take in the darkness alone. The Joybringings of autumn put them into drunken revelry for a time, but all other nights were spent in tears. The making of men that would preserve life for new generations took place always in the broad daylight of the suns, which was not ideal. But wermen above all desire to make men, by thrusting their flip into the sacred chambers of women, and it is because of this desire that the Passian race survives.

Concerning death, the Ancient Nephinarthins had a ritual most equally bizarre. When the beloved passed, and only the beloved, they would perform Pisscraft. This was a high tradition of setting up small stones in a great pit, and then urinating on them in an intricate design. The urine would then illuminate these stones— for they are of a special substance found only along the shores of Cathuma— and in this way they would honor and celebrate the legacy of the dead. Pisscraft was not performed for the demise of those vile or heinous.

The last thing we know of these ancient peoples is that they delighted in the game of Bouth, where one participant would hurl a stone directly into the mouth of another. Those who could sustain the game with the lesser loss of teeth and blood, would be proclaimed victor and given a large pot which they would then call the Victor Pot. This tradition explains why, to this day, the word victor can either denote one victorious, or simply a large pot.

For a thousand years it was so, with all that was civilization in the world huddled around one tremendous body of wave, joined around with hearth and absurd custom. Tell anyone from this Age that the future belonged to a barbaric band of outsiders, and they would swear you a tract of crow's gut. But the future winds a crooked road, and the root of all the days ahead— of all the land to East and West— began not in Nephinarthos, but off thirty miles afar.

It was a desolate rock, amidst a wide plain. Nothing lived there, not even creatures of the dust. But down from tall and misty Fingers, descended from a tribe of pure dumb savagery, a werman and his family walked. Migrating west across the Hollow Rounds, knowing not where to rest, chance took them down past this rock.

The patriarch looked upon it and knew this was to be his home.

Part One

The Kings of Therok

On Thellig

It was a mighty werman called Thellig, whom history would have indeed forgotten if it could, who gazed upon the famous stone. His deeds were unremarkable— a simple chieftain who claimed hold of a mighty rock in the waning days of the Fourth Age.

There were originally but forty members of Thellig's tribe, and the authority he commanded over even them was questionable at best. He would stand high upon the rock, where no one else could go, but this was the extent of his prowess. Soon, however, neighboring tribes caught wind of the strange man who dwelled atop the great rock, and they walked from all corners across the Plains of Hollis to gaze upon the one who commanded the rock.

To the outsiders, this man was of imposing stature. A tall brute with broad shoulders and a penetrating glance— and sharp hair all upon his face, the likes of which the people of the Plains had never seen in such volume.

In truth, it is most probably the beard that cemented the reputation of the Rock King. The beard that drew people from all winds, the beard that tickled upon the curiosities. And with tales of the tall bearded beast standing high upon the tall polished rock, where no other man could reach— indeed it was rumored that Thellig had used his mighty power to construct and place the rock himself— the tribe of forty grew into a nation upwards of four hundred.

To the modern kingdoms of man, this is but an meager village. But in the Fourth Age, a nation of four hundred was enough to form a glorious raiding party. And so Thellig and his band of strong riders rode towards the sound of the breaking waves, the same that had beckoned the Nephinarthins innumerous centuries before. There were battles along the coast, but Thellig

— although strong and fierce— was sorely matched for the organization of the Nephinarthin ranks.

His campaigns were but rosy-fingered failures.

The King of what would shortly thereafter be known as the Kingdom of Therok— a brilliant name for which nobody could possibly explain the etymology— was in all regards a hollow figure. He had single-handedly turned his tribe of forty into an army of four hundred, and then dwindled it away to a withered six.

Where Thellig's true talent lay was in the realm of child bearing. This was perhaps his one great contribution, and indeed— as earlier stated— if it were not for the deeds of his children, his name would today not have echoed a single sound into our ears. In regards to Thellig's relations, they were numerous. He would either call for women to be sent up the Rock, via means of a large horn ripped from the mouth of a horglefunt, or he would venture down into the grassy fields in the small hours of the night, to creep into tents and ravish whichever man or woman chance happened him to fall upon.

"Thellig the Ravisher" then, is what he has been to History. Ravisher not for the conquered lands to his West— for those would stand strong for another handful of generations— but for his blatant and indiscriminate use of women for his twilight deeds. The Ligian Cave depicts Thellig in his grey years with a brood of ninety-nine sons, all huddled around, adding hairs to his beard (the hairs coming from unfortunate nomads who found themselves with the boundaries of Therok). Such evidence as found in ancient caves are of no serious use when concerning concrete figures, but nonetheless we can justly assume he had numerous sons.

But then, out of these numerous sons, he had but one. For all the others perished in flame when their coach went tumbling down the stony paths of Urvenhu. Damned be the heavens, must have been the thoughts of Thellig if he had any soul at all. If nothing else, Thellig cursed the Nephinarthins, who had only just introduced the wheel and coach to Thellig. Naturally, he laid the blame of this mechanical innovation directly at the doors of the Sea-Dwellers, and went to war with them until he realized that without the use of his ninety-nine sons whom he was fighting for, he could not hope to win the fight. And if he had still had his ninety-nine sons, there would then have been no reason to fight in the first place. Thellig went home.

The other outcome of the Urvenhu Peril was that now Thellig had but one male heir. And being as this son was the only one excluded from the Hunting Party that wrought devastation for all the others, it becomes abundantly clear how Thellig thought of this child. No, this child was not excluded from the doomed party for any reason of premonition or parental protection. This child was excluded for he was in all ways an embarrassment of creation.

On Rurderlurr

Rurderlurr was not a remarkable werman. His life was marked solely by disgrace and tragedy, and— like his father— would've been absolutely forgotten by all the descendants of the world if not for an unlikely event that happened in the next generation. But as we do know a stagnant bit about the stagnant life of Rurderlurr, we will go ahead and share, for his place among the founding lineage of greatness can be ill-disputed.

Rurderlurr has come to be synonymous with tragedy, for the only records we have of his deeds concern his attraction to a certain Jelco of Medwyn, on the Shark Fin Tip of the Sea.

Being the sole surviving son of a king— albeit king of a small land in the immediate surroundings of a rock— Rurderlurr could've had his pick of any number of solitary women among Therok. Here, "any number" is in actuality somewhere along the line of fifty. But still, that is a healthy choosing pool that any man lesser than a prince would be certainly glad to pick from.

But Rurderlurr was not interested in any of the fifty or so potential suitors. His eyes were set solely on Jelco.

The old King Thellig watched in abysmal writhing as his only surviving son failed to win the affections of this pretty girl from the tip of the Sea. For Jelco did not fancy Rurderlurr in the slightest, and never would. In fact, such was Jelco's disdain of Rurderlurr, that she would tense up in fear as he would approach— hoping he would fail to see her and pass by altogether.

Thellig soon grew tired of the runaround. He forced his son Rurderlurr to take a wife from among the Therokians, whom he lined up in a crowd at the bottom of his great rock. When Rurderlurr refused— even in the midst of a hundred young ladies standing down in the rock heaps— Thellig was thereby forced to force. He poisoned Rurderlurr's cup, and the young prince went numb in all ways except for his pitiful flip.

The servants of Thellig then placed the body of Prince Rurderlurr on a large flat stone, and brought in all the women willing to lay with royal flesh, one at a time. In this way, the pitiful prince— the scourge of Thellig's eye— came to have just as many children as his fathers before, though mostly girls.

Still, Thellig rejoiced, as well as a cross old cougher might, to see that his line would continue through the blood of a grandson when the time should come. And with this one bright thought in his mind, Thellig, Father of Therok and King Upon the Rock, passed out of this world, silently. For he genuinely choked upon his own long beard, and sound is quite impossible when the airway is blocked entirely.

Upon his father's death, the first action Rurderlurr took as king was to banish all the women who had raped him.

The children stayed, but would be in need of mothers, for nearly all the women in Therok had participated in the Rape of Rurder, and hence the small country was now predominantly wermen.

To solve this dilemma, the second King of Therok sent his riders up the coast of the Sea to convince women to come to the land of wermen, off to the East in the place now called Thellig Rock. As the king's men neared the town of Medwyn, on the

Shark Fin Tip, they kept a keen eye for the lady Jelco, for the king had still had a keen heart for none but her.

Jelco hid among barrels when she heard that men of Therok had come. And with swift departures she ran out of town in the night, rathering to face weeks of weary step in walking all the way round the Sea than to come face to face with her old admirer.

When Rurderlurr heard that Jelco had fled, he sent out parties in all directions, and he himself walked around the Sea in anguish. Still, Jelco evaded them, but was eventually found living in Gizelia, almost back to where she had started.

The second King of Therok asked why she had so long eluded him. Why she would not at least have a cup with him atop his inherited rock. She responded that he was no king, but rather just the son of an ill-mannered chieftain who happened to double his following, then capture more by force and dwindle it all again through stupidity. She told him that the tongue he spoke was barbaric, and the customs of Therok were primitive beyond measure. She could never dream of having engagements with any but her own folk, the high winded and noble Nephinarthins.

Then, Jelco had questions for the king. Why had he continued to pursue her although it was made clear that she did not love him? Why would he not accept any of the women of Therok who would gladly lay with the royal flesh?

Rurderlurr responded that he had no desire for Therokian flesh what only wanted him for his power over the small rock. Indeed, his power was small— small so in that it had no weight over Jelco— but without any power at all the Therokian women would've also had no interest in him. Also, said the weeping king, he thought that if he denied all others, and stayed true to the one passion in life he felt, that one day Jelco might realize the extent of his love and find a way to reciprocate.

That way was never found. Rurderlurr lived out his life in anguish— albeit with some comfort towards the end, for his disdain of the Rock led to his establishing a more homely palace amidst the Fields to the Southwest. We now know them as the Wilderfrant Wheat Fields; they knew them as nothing more than The Fields.

It is said that the terribly lonely are fated to linger on in long, solitary days, watching from afar as all around rejoice in companionship, then together fall into dust. This has never been more true than of the isolated King Rurderlurr, of whom it is said did not speak a word for the last twenty years of his life (he lived to be well over a hundred).

It was not the place of any of the children he sired with the banished women of Therok, then, to become king. He always detested that brood, for they were tainted with rape and of his father's memory. But of his grandsons, he could be more open. So it was that when the gods finally granted mercy and brought him to the door of death, Rurderlurr held a great trial to seek out the next king from his lot of grandsons.

The Trial of Therok consisted of ninety pigs, twelve wolves, four hundred cats, and three dogs.

That is all we know.

But of Rurderlurr's lot of grandsons, which surely numbered upwards of two hundred, there was but one standing in the circle of contesters when the last moon began to set: a young werman called Francil.

And it is here that our lengthy account of the two Therokian founders is to pay off. For it was Francil that propelled the names of his fathers into eternity; Francil who turned the beleaguering nation of Therok into a glorious power that would one day unite all the peoples of the world.

On Francil

The year was 1879 when Francil dawned the Three-Sided Dagger, the emblem of Therokian kingship. There was no crown as of yet, nor did the image of a king wearing anything atop his head other than hair ever cross the minds of these folk. Kingship was only as grand as the strength you put through the sword allowed, and in this regard Francil was somewhere between Thellig and Rurderlurr.

While not as outright violent as Thellig the Ravisher, Francil could nonetheless use a blade when it was demanded of him, unlike the perpetually gentle Rurderlurr who never wrought the blood of any. But truly, it was in the theater of peace and love that Francil thrived.

Francil had a roaring passion for flowers. He would so enjoy the sights and smells of the wild weeds growing to the north in the Hills of Serco that he would sleep on his bare back under its stars from time to time. And such was his love for the blooming colors that it was he who first harvested seeds and planted foreign life around his own palace.

In this way, Francil became the Father of the Garden. The first five years of his reign— a time of peace among all Therok and with the neighboring cities in Nephinarthos— were devoted almost solely to the cultivation of gardens, to the dismay of all, who never dreamed that such heavenly oasises could exist and spring up so rapidly through the hands of man.

Apart from garden growing, the other task Francil occupied himself with in the first five years was that of finding a queen. He knew well the tragedy that had befallen his royal grandfather, and would aim hard to prevent such woe from striking himself. Thus, when the first of his affections denied his request for elopement, Francil did not despair. He would not allow his whole life to be spent chasing after the warmth of one who would likely never be swayed. And so he tried again.

Like his grandfather, it was the ladies of Nephinarthos that Francil was drawn towards. And like Jelco before, the desired ladies of Nephin Bay were never keen to accept the proposals of a Therokian. For the nation of Therok was still but a palace beside a rock, with little more than a thousand inhabitants; it had not grown in prowess nor in fame.

The Year 1884 began and Francil grew distraught. Years had passed but none whom he fancied would have him, despite his tenderness. He was but a fraction of the age of his grandfather when complete solitude had consumed him, but still he worried. For Francil had sent out flowers— magnificent flowers, harvested from all corners of the land— to all ends of the Sea, with a note attached to each, offering vast wealth and unspeakable riches to any who might come forth to join in union with the king.

All flowers were sent back, and all flowers held a note of refuse.

Shortly thereafter, Francil saw himself growing old within a matter of weeks, with nobody to share a walk through his gardens, nobody to share the warmth of his chambers.

And thus the chambers seemed to grow cold. And dusty, and damp. And Francil in the middle of the night could see his wooden walls and palace doors chipping apart and withering into ash, decaying into rot. Visions of the future, ripping down from above and obliterating the weak foundations of his fathers filled the mind of the young king.

Such was the feeble mind of Francil when an unexpected note arrived from the Far North... farther than even the great River of Andiloth, which none now living had ever claimed to cross. Any memory of land beyond the River had since been long forgotten.

Such was the surprise then, when King Francil of Therok read the letter, an invitation in fact: inviting him to cross over the Andiloth and ascend into the great mountains to the northwest, where he would receive a great gift. The taking of this great and mighty gift would lead us into The Fifth Age.

On the Crown of Ithyendor

Francil's advisors pleaded him not to go. Such a venture was folly— to cross the Andiloth into unknown territory where not a single known civilization tread, this was one thing foolhardy enough. But then to continue, and ascend the rocky cliffs that lay even further ahead? Ridiculous to the absolute.

"They mean to murder you," said all the king's men. "Such a prize isn't worth the effort, even if it is genuine— which is most certainly isn't."

But it was when Francil was told to consider all he'd be leaving behind, that he made his decision. He would indeed cross the Andiloth. For he had no family to speak of. His mother had been banished by Rurderlurr. He had been rejected by all the women he had attempted to court. And with this strongly in mind, Francil would not be swayed.

He set out with a party of fifty-sex men, towards the Andiloth. They reached the rocky barren lands near what would one day be called Arides, and looked out over the valley. The Andiloth roared wide and strong; they could not cross here.

Along the ridge they walked, through strange red canyons which subsided into flat-rocks, then into a rolling desert with bubbling black pools of tar and mud. Still the Andiloth flowed swift and relentless, and all who attempted to cross were carried off and drowned without remorse.

Here, much of the party turned back. Such was the power of Francil of the Flowers: faded, and king only in name, like his tender-hearted grandfather.

Only eleven companions remained when they reached the great Plain of Sashara, which Francil named for his favorite affection, the first to deny his proposal. Here they saw the river to be calm, and just beyond— for the land here was incredibly flat— the rising peaks of mountains in the distance could be easily spotted.

The Twelve Therokians crossed the Andiloth on a small raft, and shortly thereafter came into contact with a small tribe of those who dwelt there. Their tongue was strange, and utterly incomprehensible to the men of Therok. All that could be surmised from their speak was not, at any cost, to head for the mountains— that they were an evil place full of dreadful misgivings.

Here, six more men turned back for the familiar side of the river, but Francil would not turn back. He and his five closest comrades dove headfirst into the mountains, which Francil took to calling the Angelocs, derived from a woman of god-like quality who had raised him up in formative years.

The Angelocs defeated two of the remaining six, and after an impassioned argument, two of the final four set back down the mountain, unwilling to go any farther. Thus it was that only the two men of the strongest will went on: King Francil of the Flowers, and his scribe-boy, Fert Dooj.

For a week they survived on their final rations, but after that, more creative methods had to be employed. The next week consisted primarily of shaving off their dead skin, and enjoying every taste of that. They tried to hunt bird, for it was only birds that they found this high up the mountain, but birds are not so easily pierced by starving wermen with barely the strength to throw a twig.

And so Francil and Fert lie on their sides, in misty stone, cradling themselves amidst contractions of their hard-moaning bowels. The time had come for even the most loyal of company to refuse the Great Call. Fert would go no further.

Francil, frustrated, reminded his friend of how far he had come, and how their prize awaited them only if they strode on. To abandon the Great Call now would be to cast away all the weeks of their journey, and Fert would pay dearly for abandoning his king upon the return to Therok. But the scribe-boy could speak no more.

As Fert lie dying, Francil turned and continued the upward ascent with all his hunger. It would take all the solitude he could muster to stumble upon what he was looking for.

Here, we can but speculate. For numerous were the days that Francil spoke of it, but always in riddle. Always in code, and always in shadow. It would change upon every occasion, the way he described their meeting. But all that is truly important, is that they did meet.

Francil, the King of Therok. And the Manes of Ithyendor. Francil called them benevolent, but with a cursing nature, as if they meant no harm yet held a foreboding of inevitable damnation within their very beings. They were otherworldly, though they did not claim to come from below the earth. Therefore they were not gods nor creatures of the Margonathi who dwelled in the center of the world since its conception. And they were not Starlings, for they were not born of a watery wooded fountain. Rather, these Manes told Francil that they came from above.

They offered him a crown. The grandest of which would ever be seen in any generation of the world, onto the dying day of the Moon. To Francil, any crown would've been a wonder to behold. For none of the lands east of the Sea had ever adorned their heads with precious metals, and this was altogether something greater.

The Crown of Ithyendor, as the Manes called it, was not of mere sparkling silver, mixed with the perfect amount of shining gold to give it a remarkably even consistency. Neither was it merely a brilliant culmination of radiant jewels that glistened lightly and from all sides, tantalizingly gorgeous. Nay, it was all of these combined, with fifty-six sharpened spikes thrusting up from the rim.

There were voices that seemed to come from within. And when one looked into the prime jewel atop the central spike— a diamond of impossible perfection— one might swear they saw passing shades of ancient faces. The faces were not elderly, but rather trapped in time, from days before the earliest tales.

With the taking of the crown, the Manes spoke also of a prophecy to be received jointly, that would bear ill for the kingdom that Francil would found. But Francil had come too far and endured too much to turn down the offer; he would resolve to found a kingdom with the glorious crown despite the foretellings of any prophecy.

Thus Francil at last took hold of the crown of the Manes, after spending seven days in their company, and never once speaking. For in their presence, he said, he had lost not only the will to speak, but the ability. As if his tongue had ceased to exist at all.

And as he descended the slope of Tall Angeloc, upon a path that the Manes had created just for him, he glowed pale with a frozen expression. The Manes whispered after him the Prophecy that they had promised:

"This device we give to you, Francil of the Flowers, to awaken the power of lordship over many men, that together all these may unite in a strength unbroken, to erect trembling towers high above ground. Your new kingdom will outlast you long: 500 years will it reign. To you this might sound an eternity, but to those who rise in those days long ahead, they will feel the curse and the sting of these words. They will fight to their end, but perish under a gathering smoke. And after the 500 years, none but the Crown will live on. For it shall reign as the true power in all this land for another span of time, the same as your kingdom, and in this way the days of our Crown are numbered at a thousand years. Once the thousand years are spent, its light will go out. Along with all who remember your name."

His body stiff, the legs of Francil carried him down the Angelocs if his body were a machine. On the way down, he passed the corpse of Fert, who for a single moment arose. Francil looked back at him, with the Crown of Ithyendor atop his head, as if to show off what destiny Fert might have shared.

Red clouds of storm and cyclone formed over the Angelocs, creating the most magnificent sky to be seen from the Plain of Sashara, where the two men who had turned back from the mountains now camped along the Andiloth. They had rested here for the last week, taking advantage of the foreign women to be found along the banks, and indulging in the dramatic nightfalls that bless the region.

On this night, they were beyond belief when their king drifted across the water, wearing the most incredible craft they had ever seen, atop his head. They looked upon him bewildered. Francil said nothing. The next day they set out for Therok.

The return journey was not filled with talk, as had been the first days of the adventure. Something heavy weighed upon Francil, both physically and in spirit. The Crown of the Manes surely lie behind both.

The palace at Therok was filled with noblemen who had either turned back from Francil's voyage or who had chosen never to set out in the first place. Those who stayed back had done so with the clear objective of harvesting their own power in the absence of the king, who it was said would surely not return. And as fellow companions returned one by one, telling of the treacherous road to the far mountains, it become certain that Francil would be no more.

Francil overheard this talk among his peers as he sat, disguised and cloaked, within his halls. This was not yet the time to reveal himself.

Instead, he set out again for Nephinarthos. There, he met with the Keeper of the Seaside Sanctuary and secured it for a grand night of fellowship and ceremony— it was to be a night in honor of the return of the king. The entire nation of Therok was invited, as were nobles and councilmen from all cities of the Sea, even as far as Cathumas.

The night of the Return Feast commenced, and Francil was nowhere to be seen. All drank and ate in the presence of great long tables, and patiently awaited the arrival of the king, whilst chatting and gossiping amiably.

Near midnight, Francil finally walked in, draped in glistening white robes. This was to be the new image of his kingdom. Gone was the rugged picture of Thellig, the warrior chieftain who lived upon a rock, and gone was the thought of pitiful Rurderlurr, weak and penniless.

How Francil's affections looked up to him now. Any one of them, he gathered by the looks in their eyes, might now have him. And so Francil walked along the aisles between the long tables... and, working his way up to it, knelt before the seat of Sashara, who always was his favorite. Once again he asked for her favor.

But Sashara, remembering the affair of the Flowers, said that she would only be courted by one who truly loved only her. Glancing around, she pointed out all who she knew of that had received a flower from Francil, and all made known that they had felt only as one amidst a group of eighty, instead of one and only one.

Francil recoiled. He said that his grandfather had put all his hope and affection in one beauty long ago, and thus he was lonely til the end of his days.

"So too, shall you be," spoke Sashara, "If you split all your hope and affection in eighty different ways. Your hope and affection is so diminished that it could never amount to anything."

Francil nodded, under the watchful eyes of all in the sanctuary. If he were to continue on after this night, his life would be nothing more than embarrassed misery on each road he walked.

And so it was to be that everyone in the hall that night perished.

Short and simple, we could leave it at that. But questions are sure to arise, after such a broad-ended statement. Was it really everyone in attendance that perished? Was it Francil that killed them? Yes, no, yes, and no.

Upon realizing that no power of words could change his circumstance for the better, Francil did the easy thing and placed his newly gifted crown atop his head. It bedazzled all, until it began to bereave them of breath.

Violently began to shake the heads of those who looked upon it. Blood shot out from the most unlikely of places; places from which blood was never known to willingly protrude. Smoke filled the room, followed by fire— or the other way around, as is likely, but survivors swore the smoke swung first.

Those who escaped the gaze of the crown hid under tables, and spoke of an even more curious fate among those closest to Francil. Sparks of blue and white jagged lines, like those seen on stormy nights in the sky, threaded the bones of momentarily illuminated skull. The ground did not shake, as is often the description from those who are lazy in their tellings. Rather, the ground cracked a whip, or fired an arrow— pulling back a great distance, and then snapping forward with tremendous force, flinging those who meant to escape into splintered wood and rising flame.

What was Francil doing throughout all of this? Casting down spells from the heavens, cursing the names of those who had abandoned his cause?

Not at all. He simply stood in one place, and amidst the madness, took a seat. He set the Crown of Ithyendor on a stool before him. Seeing the crown unguarded, one of the burning nobles took hold of it, as if to stop the horror. But upon laying hands on it, they burst off. The crown refused to be handled.

Of the hundreds gathered in the sanctuary that night, only fourteen escaped onto the beach. They scattered and ran, to all corners of civilization, exclaiming the terror that the King of Therok wielded. When asked if there should be an army raised to counter the Crown, they said it would be useless. No power could stand in the breast of it. Within days, all the survivors succumbed to a horrifying sickness, after turning pale green and then rotting away from the inside out.

The memory of the night in Nephinarthos would last for centuries. Indeed, it would be another five hundred years until that the Crown of Ithyendor need even be spoken outright in its full title. For all knew of its power, all knew of its devastating impact.

For the rest of his reign, Francil tucked his crown away in a safe box, seven layers thick and locked hard with precious metals. All men feared him, and all men would now follow him to whatever end. That end would take them back towards the Andiloth, for Francil refused to stay in his old country. It bred nothing but ill memories of an unhappy past. So it was that the gardens were overgrown, the palace deserted, and Thellig's Rock abandoned.

The Nation of Therok would establish itself anew, on the banks of the Andiloth, overlooking the Angelocs, where Francil and his brave followers had crossed the river on to an uncertain fate the previous year.

Francil gave to his new kingdom the name of Angelon, and the grand city at its core Angelon Othim, which grew faster than any city along the Sea ever did. In his heart, Francil knew it was out of fear— for fear of his terrible gift— that people flooded to his court. He knew that when he was a young and simple king, he had been rejected by all. But this Crown that he kept locked in a chest had unchained hell upon hundreds.

"So this is what makes them follow," laments a crumbling statue of Francil in a famous fountain, still to be seen in the oldest courtyard of ruined Angelon Othim to this day.

Francil of the Flowers would rule another fifty years, until the year 1935, when he attempted to murder himself with a knife to the throat. He was quickly revived by his physicians, who then brought in a twelve-year-old girl, so that the line of the king might be preserved (Francil had never sought out a wife after the dark night at the Seaside Sanctuary).

The girl, called Semerau, conceived, and upon the news, Francil took a second knife to the throat, this time bleeding out so fast that none could stitch him fast enough.

On Penflath and Vicar

And that brings us to the mighty King Penflath. The word mighty here being completely out of place and to be snickered at the thought of using it, for Penflath was anything but. As a king he was utterly insignificant— there is but one thing that can be said of his reign.

This singular thing is that pickles were invented in his time as king, and even this, chroniclers believe, has been attributed to him for lack of anything else existing as testament to his own existence. Instead of endlessly speculating, then, on what could have possibly transpired during the reign of this young king—we will not and simply pass right through it.

If Penflath was boring and able to be hopped over in the mind of the chronicler, his son was anything but. Born simply with the name Marc, he would endow himself with a long list of others as his days mounted, with history finally settling on calling him Grand Marc Vicar. Indeed, he preferred the title "grand" over "king," for he believed it set him apart. Any man could be a king (if you were descended from one of course); his dull father Penflath and great-great grandfather Rurderlurr had been kings. But Marc Vicar was to be something more.

He was to be a lism flok of mikkin darb fute.

(I have sworn to taking use of profane language in this manuscript ever so sparingly, but one must excuse me for here using five of our worst profanities in one phrase. For it is certainly demanded when speaking of the third King of Angelon and the fifth and final king of the pure Therokian Line.)

To spell the deeds of Grand Marc Vicar is to paint a wall of gushing blood and severed vein, with snapping bone and entrail slain.

His own grandfather Francil, who murdered hundreds in one night with the Crown of Ithyendor, would be appalled at the rashness of Marc Vicar. His grandfather to the third, Thellig the Ravisher, would be taken back by his unprovoked acts of violence.

Enough with the broad talk and onto specifics. Grand Marc Vicar was concerned with conquest, and as he looked upon the map and saw that his fathers had commanded Thellig Rock, and he himself controlled the rapidly growing Angelon Othim, it seemed only right that he should take the entire Sea of

Cathuma into his dominion. He held councils at the halls of Nephinarthos, but those in attendance— remembering the evil night of the Sanctuary— were not prepared to enter into any deal with a descendant of Francil. Marc Vicar reminded them that he was still in possession of the Crown, to which the Nephinarthins smartly rebuked that he would never dream of using it.

This was, in fact, right. As heinous a man as Grand Marc Vicar would grow to become, he would not once open the great chest containing the Crown of Ithyendor. And the Nephinarthins knew this, for it was common talk that the Angelon Council who had ruled in Marc Vicar's name throughout his childhood had imparted into him a great fear of the Crown. They spared no details in describing to the child all the horrors that befell those in the Seaside Sanctuary that night long ago, and the stories naturally terrified the young Marc Vicar. It was firmly implanted in his mind that the Crown was only to be used in the time of the Finishing, and might very well only respond to the touch of a demon's hand.

So the Nephinarthins, knowing Marc Vicar would not use the dreaded Crown against them, made the fatal mistake of resistance. They did not assume that Marc Vicar would descend upon their lands with every other means of human torture imaginable.

He did.

The King of Angelon that called himself Grand Marc Vicar annihilated all the cities along the Sea, effectively ending then and forever the Golden Age of Nephinarthos. Never again would their culture rise to play a prominent role in world dealings. They were smashed, obliterated, by the broad iron gloves that he wore as he rode his black and red spotted horse along sand beaches, holding a large mace in his right and a four-bladed sword in his left.

For the peoples of Nephinarthos, Grand Marc Vicar devised a very particular manner of execution. The wermen, from the age of 28 to 56, would be slaughtered by sword on the battlefields where they stood. The battlefields were, of course, the city streets which Marc Vicar raided without warn. All wermen under the age of 28 were allowed an arrow, pierced through the throat (the archers would hit their mark every time, and if this is to believed then Grand Marc Vicar had truly assembled the greatest force of archers seen for several ages). Those over the age of 56 were cast into the sea, which was called mercy.

For the women, whom Marc Vicar despised for their humiliating of Francil, and for what he proclaimed the long-passed-over sins of Jelco, he set ablaze in their basins. "Baths of fire, pure flame all the same, for the punctilious peoples," he cried fiercely, eventually turning it into a song of aggravation.

Those who could escape found their way to the only place Vicar would not dare follow: the Sashite Mountains— thick, dense, and impenetrable, far taller and more rocky than the Angelocs. These lie to the southwest of the Sea, and stretch on for hundreds of miles. The descendants of some original Nephinarthins could still be found here in the Eleventh Age, amidst other peoples, in the long-running mountains that also derive their names from the lovely affection of Francil.

Back along the Nephin Bay, Vicar razed all temples and homes, all shops and makeries. What he replaced them with was far less, for the architects and builders of Angelon Othim were not yet on par with the Nephinarthins, who had practiced stonework for the past thousand years.

If there is one thing that Marc Vicar did contribute to which is of any use to us today, it is the Ligian Cave, which was of his doing. It is the oldest source of knowledge we have found concerning the deeds of Thellig and Rurderlurr. Knowledge which comes at the price of forgetting the more elaborate histories of Classical Nephinarthos, which we are told originally adorned the Cave Walls, but were overwritten by Marc Vicar, with the tales he deemed more appropriate for the dawning Age of Angelon.

In this Age of Angelon, Vicar envisaged himself ruling all the land from north of the River Gizle and the Sashite Mountains, west to the River Swifting and north to the Green Woods. If one regards a map, they will find that this dream of Marc Vicar's took almost all of Eleventh Age Ilandia under his eye, save Soshattaron and Dunland.

The early 1980s held a long string of victory for Grand Marc Vicar. With his scourge of archers of axe-men he rode from Gizelia to Melas Nostras, the great fire fields on the border of the Green Woods. It looked as though certainly none could stop him on this side of the world.

Then it was for those west of the Sashites to try.

Part Two

The Line of Hendik

On Rosy King Hanna

For long did the peoples of Nephinarthos wonder what lie in the unmapped regions of Denderrin Othim. They dwelled not long on it, however, for they had not the men to carry out such a vast venture, nor the men to necessitate it.

The folk of blossoming Angelon were soon to find out a bit of what that distance held, though, for an amiable pot-bellied king was soon to pop up on the front of Marc Vicar's ambitions. This was Rosy King Hanna, who approached Vicar on a black field near Seventh Age Baracoe in the year 1984, with a wink and a whistle of whimsy. Marc Vicar might have drawn his sword through the Rosy King then and there, if it weren't for his unbelievable manners and tales. He was of a naturally white complexion— though not nearly as white as Dikenians— with spotted skin and a deep red rash on his face, that he said was only a result of the burning sun, which was not so bright (indeed, hardly ever seen) in his country. This did not stop the Angelons from christening him "The Rosy King." And indeed he was so called rosy for when he got excited his face would turn pink as raw foreskin.

Grand Marc Vicar had undoubtedly grown tired of the Rosy King of Hendik shortly after laying eyes on him, but his rope truly snapped after King Hanna had been two years in the hospitality of Angelon Othim, relating all the lands and customs of his country to the chroniclers.

Legend speaks of a broad jar filled to brim with fly-honey, the sacred nectar of the folk in the Hollow Rounds. Starting with the founding of Angelon Othim, this fly-honey had been brought in as a delicacy, given as a gift to the Mighty Francil ere he wage war against the cavern-dwellers of the Hollow Rounds. Fit for only the royal line, the gift of the fly-honey was spread to the offspring of the third-born of any given king. This, however, was not meant to include kings of foreign country.

This, then, would be enough to thoroughly redden the face of Grand Marc Vicar, who is said to have caught the Rosy King butt-nude in the Angelon cellars, dancing before a deep bathwater basin. Imagine his further infuriation, then, to find his fifteen-year-old daughter in the tub, also nude— laughing aside the Rosy King with streaks of fly-honey all over her wetted flesh. One could imagine that Marc Vicar would be obligated to undergo another hue-change upon this second rude discovery, and so it is said his face turned from rash red to ashen black.

Of course we can never say for certain what led Marc Vicar to the forcing out of Rosy King Hanna; indeed the aforementioned tale reeks of sensationalism. What we find most likely is that Marc Vicar simply ran a draught in his patience well, as is typically the case after long harboring an unwelcome guest. Indeed, those who side with the Rosy Line heartily rebuke the story of the fly-honey, for they say it would be for Hanna— though jolly and merry of love-making— highly out of character to seduce the daughter of his kingly host, especially one so young.

Regardless, Hanna was expelled from the gates of Angelon Othim in 1986, and wandered the Andiloth Plains for some time thereafter. This continued to shed displeasure into the life of Marc Vicar, who had surely assumed the Rosy King would depart back for his homelands after expulsion from the Angelon capital. But still he lingered, roaming from town to town in a laughing band of campers, spreading the joy of Hendik lore.

To speak to all the intricacies of Ancient Hendik mythos would be to warrant an entire other book on its own, so we will tell of only the roots, and that which many find to be most essential: the Noble Stocks of Gwidenarsa.

Among these were the Chipperins, little winged creatures of the woods who would whisper lewd obscenities to those abstaining from allurement.

There were Ekwins, great crosses between bear and man, with four legs and two arms, and in their belly pockets harboring eyes, some with teeth.

There were Beasts of the Gar Loly, which consisted of nothing more than long tentacles that would climb slowly up and down trees, wise beyond the understand of men.

And of course one would be amiss without mentioning the Beings of Kooskan Parse, they being many-fingered faces resting between the clamps of two sharp radiant shells, which would move as wheels to give them haste.

But last and greatest of these, there were Starlings. For these were bred by Tiluma himself, as will be told in the Third Part of this manuscript. These had since grown scarce in the presence of the world, but at least they were still to be found on its surface. For the other legendary beings of the West— though sworn to still grace the land by Rosy King Hanna— were thoroughly proven shortly thereafter to have been dispelled for the earth long ago, if they had ever existed to begin with. For they are beasts to harbor the minds of children, and remain solely in the legendary tales of that place.

Nonetheless, the peoples of Angelon knew none the better. And so these were the things Rosy King Hanna spoke off around fire, with bottle in hand, to wonderstruck folk. His charismatic telling of strange tales and an even stranger world captivated these peoples, and the mythos spread wildly. So much so that Grand Marc Vicar grew concerned for his own position as king. True, the Rosy King had always annoyed him— even more so when his carefree culture began to permeate into the strict step of his own— but after three years, the people of Angelon came to love King Hanna so much that Marc Vicar could feel the supplanting of his reign not far off.

In the year 1989, Marc Vicar sent out a stealthy force towards the Kingdom of Hendik, to gather all the knowledge it could. It was two-weeks' ride from Angelon Othim to the Hendik fortress of Greencastle, or so King Hanna had claimed.

It took the Angelon riders two months. And those are the lucky ones we speak of; those who didn't finally happen upon the path are probably still out searching. The road was through a dense, previously unexplored forest: The Green Woods, as they were immediately named by the men of Angelon, for the blatant notice of its abundance in the color green. To any of my readers who hail from the western reaches of Elaptirius— Stonearch, Ockland, and Excelsior in particular— you may have come to take the color green for granted. In Nephinarthos, in Therok, in Angelon— hardly any natural occurrences of green were to be found in these places. Any instances of green trees or grass that you might be familiar with there are the result of a later age.

So imagine the enthrallment of these Angelon riders then, who perhaps had never even seen a tint of gentle green in their nighttime fantasies, when they reached the end of the Black Fields, and saw an endless line of trees spreading east and west, with tops of the most vibrant, delectable green that ever existed on the face of Tiluma's wide world. Imagine their further enthrallment, then, as they tried to figure out a way to break into the forest.

Some gave up quickly and tried for alternate routes— only to learn quickly after that the northern wall of the Sashites is just as impassable, if not more so. Some of the Angelons considered asking the Hendiks how they had managed to navigate the dense forest on their way into Angelon, but then they remembered they were spies in the service of Marc Vicar, not to reveal any hint of their mission.

In the end, the Angelon riders left their horses for dead amidst the tangled trees, and on foot they were able to cross over into the Western Green Woods, with its high and noble palms being much more forgiving than the horrific mesh of any-tree found on the eastern side of the Woods. After a week of wandering without map, for none existed, many of them had a sinking suspicion that they were all traveling about in circles. This is primary evidence, for they are the exact words of the dead who were later on found starved to death.

But, as earlier stated, those who Fortune winked upon found their way through the Green Woods, some even claiming to have had encounters with the mystical Starlings that Rosy King Hanna spoke so highly of. They made it to Hendik, to Greencastle, and did their spying for the jealous king.

News came much too late for the taste of Marc Vicar upon his throne in Angelon Othim. Indeed, the year was almost up, and his riders brought back nothing of strategic importance. For Marc Vicar had wondered who was ruling Rosy King Hanna's realm of Hendik in his stead, if anyone. Marc Vicar hoped that he might possibly dissolve Hanna's kingdom into his own, and then execute the fat and pink king. But news of Hendik proved otherwise: the country was thriving under Hanna's four sons, who miraculously enough were able to divide their lands peacefully and prosper off of one another (something that has never since been successfully duplicated by ruling sons).

Marc Vicar foamed at the mouth and had his scribe-boy collect the foam as evidence of his wrath, to be stored in the Royal Gallery until the end of time. He then declared a bounty on the Rosy King— a newly created position, the Minister of Deeds, would be granted to the one who brought in Hanna with entrails bound round his neck and testicles stuffed up his nostrils.

Many in the kingdom coveted the title, but none wanted to kill Rosy King Hanna. So in the waning weeks of 1989, Marc Vicar received corpse after corpse, with entrails bound round the neck and testicles shoved up the nose, but he knew none of them to be Hanna. Close enough resemblances for a fool, but a fool not was he.

Marc Vicar then declared outright war upon all of Hendik. He searched every stone in Angelon for its leader, but in vain— the Rosy King had returned to Greencastle to alert his own people of what had come to piss. He intended to take the fight directly back to the Vicar, and to rid the people of Angelon from their heinous king.

The first blows came in 1991, when the armies of Angelon and Hendik met on the edge of the Green Woods, with the River Swifting between them. Here, the Angelocs had a great advantage, for the silly Hendiks had only rudimentary tools for launching projectiles. Sadly, the vast majority simply resorted to throwing rocks with their hands. And while they did this, the Angelocs fired volley after volley with their deadly bows, the arrows of which were made from pure Tiplood (the sharpest natural substance we know of) and crafted with care to be both ornamentally and tactically superb in ripping through the hearts of men.

And so this incident on the banks of the Swifting was not pleasant for the Hendiks.

From here on, the Rosy King chose his battles by not choosing them, and avoiding the Angelon army at all costs. He preferred to attack the king's villages by night, taking them by surprise or through theatrical trickery. The ancient towns of Frawlin, Lucilian, and Urna Noht were all taken in this manner.

Marc Vicar at last managed to catch one of the Rosy Family, the eldest prince of Hendik, a man called Bennion. As Marc Vicar's prisoner, Bennion was treated cruelly, as could be expected. I will not delve into specific methods of torture, for I have found that the spreading of procedural torture only leads to such procedures being eagerly revived, and it is the goal of my friends in this new Twelfth Age to eradicate all of it forever.

Apologies for the slight divergence into the present. But Bennion of Hendik, son of King Hanna, was in the custody of

Grand Marc Vicar, and word of this spread quickly. A letter arrived bearing the signature of Hanna, asking what his demand might be. Marc Vicar declared to all the land that Prince Bennion of Hendik would be brutally executed, for all the city of Angelon Othim, if the Rosy King did not agree at once to a fair battle.

And so Marc Vicar finally had his rival in his grip. Hanna of Hendik gave up his game of Hide and Strike, and chose a rounded clearing in the Western Green Woods, dipping down from the rest of the forest floor, as the location for the fight. The spot would be known forever after as Battlewood.

On Naegeli

The Battle of Battlewood might best be described as muddied. For the rains are quite prevalent in this corner of the Green Woods, and the soil always deep with grabbing gush. So as the charges commenced, horse and man hoof alike were slowed to an exerted stomp, and with every downing of boot the ground would become more upset. Men fell upon their faces quickly, for they longed to charge swiftly, without realizing their pies to be still held by the thick muds. Soldiers on both side lashed out in frenzied curses, and the mud was thrown up from the earth.

In this way, much of the battle transpired with the outfits of all being so thickly coated in earth that none could tell who was on the side of whom. And mud covered the eyes as well, so that the best any could do was to swing a sword with full strength and pray to Athrallia that it might bite the neck of an adversary. Screams and wails sounded out so loud that any attempt to command the battle were wholly without fruit. In this way, the victory cannot be attributed to Marc Vicar, nor the loss to Hanna, for the battle was nothing more than a clashing of armored beasts.

When at last all men were cast to the ground, unable to stand for their legs had been hacked off in all instances, Grand Marc Vicar rode forth from his position. He had not fought that day, but rather waited beyond view, so that his life would be preserved in any case. As he waded among the dead and dying, he had servants knelt constantly at his side, to remove the mud before it coated his boots. He searched the bodies of all until he found the five he was looking for: the Rosy King of Hendik, along with his four sons. All had been slaughtered and dismembered.

Marc Vicar did not celebrate, nor present his men with a victorious grin. Rather, he rode back to his capital with a barren expression, thinking only that this day should have transpired years prior. He was rid of his burden from the west, and all his male heirs had been dealt with in the same chilling manner.

That night, Marc Vicar sat upon his throne, for this is where he slept, ever upright and watchful across his hall. But on this particular night, following the slaughter of Battlewood, he heard a creaking of wood. The solemn king rose and walked about, searching for the the creaking by candlelight. At last he stood over the source, and looked down.

To his great surprise, a voice spoke up to him. "Kindly King of Angelon, I am but trapped under these floor boards. If you could assist me in my plight I would be forever grateful, and you would be of rich reward." The voice belonged to that of a trembling young woman.

"How is it that you came to be trapped under my floorboards?" Questioned the tired king.

"It was the doing of ghastly King Hanna, who kept me as his slave for all his long years in your country."

Here Marc Vicar grew angered at the mention of Hanna's name, but remembered him and his sons to be lying dead in Battlewood, and so pressed the girl on, bidding her to speak to all of the Rosy King's atrociousness.

"He is atrocious beyond all measure, my lord," continued the girl beneath the floorboards. "He is vile, boar-faced, and deserving of any terrible fate that Trankle Plooce might deliver him."

Here at last Marc Vicar formed a small grin, with remained unseen by the girl, for she was under floorboards. "It is true that Trankle Plooce did deliver a mighty terrible fate to that werman on this day, but do continue."

And so for nine hours the girl was made to become redundant, speaking ill word upon the dead King of Hendik to delight the jealous King of Angelon for all the night. She had soon used up all the words in existence that were synonymous with heinous, and then began to make up words that fit the same purpose. Finally Marc Vicar let out an uproarious cackle, and the girl then demanded that she be let out from the floorboards.

Tired and truly ready for sleep, Marc Vicar said that the job would require the word of wood-cutters after he had slept. But the girl said that the job was easily done— there was a hole in one of the planks and all that needed doing was for Marc Vicar to kneel down and lift up on the plank-hole. Vicar at last consented and knelt down, but when he put his fingers through the plank-hole, they were grabbed clamped upon by shears. Then did the girl erupt from the floor, holding the king's fingers in a grip and twisting him round, so that she ended atop his back, sending him to the floor with fingers ripping off in the fall.

This girl now sat on the top of Mac Vicar's shoulders, and with iron gloves sent his head smashing into the wooden floor repeatedly, but not hard enough to knock the king from awareness. Bewildered beyond all ends, Grand Marc Vicar looked into the dark, seeing only the iron glove that clenched his throat, and asked, "Who of all foul lords bred you?"

"I am Naegeli, born of tall blood just as you, my home lying under the skies of Hendik. Though now my home shall be this — for the life departs you, Cosh Marc. Just as you allowed my father and my brothers to be slaughtered without ceremony, so shall I slaughter you."

And she put her knife up behind the lips of Marc Vicar, cutting the roof of the gums and then proceeded to carve every tooth, which she then placed under the eyelids of the ravenous king.

For the killing blows, she slowly drove her knife straight up Vicar's urethra, and then battered his face in with her ass.

Thus was the passing of Grand Marc Vicar, and as he was discovered the next morning, no one questioned the departure. All his ministers had despised him, and so the cause of death was ruled to be an accident of the late hours, for often are the times when one might rise in the middle of night and come to mistakenly mutilate themselves.

Debates had just begun to rumble for who would rise to succeed Marc Vicar, who had no heir, when a lovely young woman resembling King Hanna arrived in the Grand Hall.

"My name is Naegeli, and I am the daughter of your beloved fart, he who was slain but days ago in a dark wooded start. Before laying down his life, he sent me here, so that I might contest for the throne should he or my brothers perish. Both have come to pass, so I swear to embody their spirits and mass, and hold in my arms their hands, should you noble folk allow me to take charge of these lands."

Many of the nobles were wary, but in the end, the tremendous love for Rosy King Hanna won out. His awful fate did much to propel the claim of his daughter, for the Angelons now felt that something was owed to the remnant of his kin. And so Naegeli, daughter of Hanna, was crowned with the Crown of Ranthir, for that of Ithyendor was still locked tightly away, so that its dreadful power might not serve as temptation to any.

Immediately after her coronation, King Naegeli began to search for a fitting groom that would cement her claim to the throne and ensure the legitimacy of her reign. Attention would have no doubt been pointed elsewhere, such as to the crumbling problems of the realm inward and outward, but Naegeli was a practical woman on all fronts, and knew that she would not rule long if the people could not find a superficial reason to support her.

And so she approached Toom, nephew of the late Grand Marc Vicar. She offered him a band of marriage, and silly Toom assumed that he would then become. But Naegeli assured him that no— he would not be king. He would serve as the quoren — that is, the consort of the king— in the same fashion as the wives of past werman kings had served as queens. It took a hefty amount of explaining for Toom to come to an understanding of the simple proposal, but he did indeed accept the proposal, for the alternative was that he would be exiled to the sea and set adrift.

The wedding occurred swiftly, and Naegeli could rest easy thereafter, knowing that she had joined the two royal lines in matrimony and thus in the minds of the people, and her place as reigning monarch was secured. She then could turn to work on matters she considered to be more pressing.

The Kingdom of Angelon was in utter disrepair after the tumultuous years of Marc Vicar. Many of his vile mercenaries still rode across plain and hill unchallenged, and to combat this disturbance, Naegeli would need to find creative means of ending their injustice. She turned to warrior tribes of Dikenia, fierce men who stuck to their lands far in the East. Naegeli became the first Angelon king to visit this distant land, and she brought with her offerings of both women and wermen, to be slave to the Dikenian warlords should they not assist willingly. This is what came to pass, and the pale-skinned Dikenians took in many Angelons as perpetual servant, on the condition that they ride west and relentlessly destroy Marc Vicar's force of mercenaries.

With this accomplished, a firm foundation of basic peace could then be re-established. But peace was not sufficient to the vast population of Angelons, who now wanted justice on top of that. For they had been wronged to great lengths by the policies of Marc Vicar as well, which had granted all their lands into to the hands of their neighbors, just to cause discontent. But now many of the Angelons had come to appreciate their new lands, with just as many craving their old lands, and so dispute erupted on all sides, and all matters were brought before King Naegeli.

Where Naegeli's successors were succeed in the appointment of men to carry out royal tasks that proved too tiresome, Naegeli succeeded in somehow managing to tackle all the tasks herself.

She did not sleep but in stretches of well-drainings, and she did not take time for her own pleasure until the trials of land and lordship were all dealt with.

Soon, though, restless Naegeli would find her relentless energy to be interrupted by an inevitable disturbance for one who wished to create a long line of offspring. This disturbance was pregnancy itself, which began to take a toll on Naegeli's body in the early months of 1996. She still made use of all hours of the day, riding all across her realm and dealing with issues of law, coin and trade, but she felt as though half of her powers were drained from the living beast inside of her.

When the child was at last liberated from its womanly hold in the spring, Naegeli did two things. Firstly, she named the child Raedym, for he was a bright-eyed boy and she always loved that name when it referred to bright-eyed boys. Secondly, she decided that she would never again have an infant of any kind grow inside of her and come bursting out. She also decided that she wanted about twenty more children. Some might see this as a problem. But King Naegeli of Angelon had an unforeseen well of resourcefulness at her fingertips.

Royal Naegeli took a carriage one morning, out of the city, heading north for the Andiloth. She crossed the river and traversed the Plains of Sashara, delving deep into the wooded valley at the foot of the Angelocs. Here she ordered plenty of provisions from the neighboring villages, and recruited experienced mountain men, for she was to make the climb.

Like Francil one Weethotial (or 112 years) prior, Naegeli swept up into the mountains, in hopes of coming into contact with the Manes of Ithyendor. She found them quite easily, for they had in turn been seeking her out. They were surprised to learn that the line of Francil had been already ended.

"Yes, it only takes one piss-eyed king to ruin it for all those in line after him," spoke Naegeli frankly. "Though it's only skipped a generation— Penflath's great-grandson will be king in his own time, for Toom son of Penflir is the father."

"Have you come only to share with us your new marriage and kin?"

"Not just to share, but to ask for your wisdom on a certain fork in my desires. See, I wish to have many children. I wish to create a tree of branching offspring that will run my name down streams of time, and I wish to place a good many of them on thrones of their own. Though I do not wish to have these children growing inside of me, for I as a king of a great nation have much work to do. Also, I wish to have much intercourse, for I greatly enjoy it."

The Manes looked on, puzzled, for perhaps the first time in all their eternal existence.

"I know it's a stumper, but there's got to be something you can do. You're the things that made a crown of lighting and fire, what's capable of making earthquakes and turning folk into dry bone."

At which point the Manes inquired where the Crown of Ithyendor lie at that moment, and Naegeli assured them that it was locked in the most sacred of chests in her palace at Angelon Othim, only to be used in the most dire of times. With this assurance, the Manes gave her their approval of her abrupt seizure of the Angelon monarchy, and granted her swift assistance in her desire to have many children, much sex, and never bear pregnancy again.

They presented her with a portable stone chamber, connected to a swirling colored shell made into a large horn, pulsating with vibrant purity and seeming to have stars reflected in the smoother surfaces. With this, Naegeli would cusp her naked holy directly after conception, and the shell horn would suction up the life from within, and in the stone chamber would grow the child just as if it were the mother's womb. Half a year would go by and, when ready, the stone chamber would emit a soft vapor, signifying the first breaths of Naegeli's new baby.

Raekal was the first to be born in this way, and he came in the early days of 1997. Naegeli was overjoyed at the ease of which her second son was brought into the world, and to celebrate her great joy, she had intercourse directly after. She didn't even wait for the rising of the moon, or to make sure that the werman she had chosen was her husband. Indeed, it wasn't.

The father of Naegeli's third child would be the man of fine craft that pulled the weeds from the fountains, and nothing is known to history of him except for this occupation. Truly, his craft must have been truly fine to attract King Naegeli to grant him this great royal honor. And their daughter would not be shamed to a life of bastardom, but she too— like her older brothers— would rise to a throne of her own. The child's name was Naemela.

Naegeli produced twenty-some other children in her life, all the rest using the same fabled Stone Chamber of the Manes, but these are not so important as to warrant any mention in this book. Only the first three became royal rulers in their own right. So we will leave it at that, and suffice to say that King Naegeli always had a child cooking in her chamber, at all times until her dying day.

In 2006 she made her second son Raekal— then only nine years old— a king of his own land, which she simply ripped apart from her own dominion. The newly carved land was to be called Enceloth, constituting the northeastern corner of the kingdom. Raekal was to be lord of that land in perpetuity, with his own offspring holding direct claim to it after his death.

To ensure that future generations would not potentially grow arrogant or lustful, Naegeli placed a burden on Enceloth: the kings would forever be known as "Lesser Kings," and each year would pay tribute to High Kings of Angelon and acknowledge a portion of their army as a conditional contingent provided for by the more ancient realm.

Around the same time, she played with the notion of carving out another chunk of her kingdom and giving it to her eldest daughter, Naemela. King Naegeli was advised against it, however, for if she carried through she would run the risk of granting away all her many lands to her children, thus fracturing her land into tiny splinters and losing all sense of grandeur that came with her now-great territories. So she held off gifting away lands to her children, and held her powers in absolute, except for the land of Enceloth, which had already been given to her son Raekal and which was currently being governed by a set of hand-picked regents.

All was glorious in Angelon for a span of sun turns, until the rascal Toom began to thirst for power. He asked if he might share in the ruling of kingdoms, along with his wife, but Naegeli shook her head and smiled. "Toom is no name for a king. Be content to be my quoren."

But Toom was not content.

Early on a bright morning then, King Naegeli and her son Prince Raedym rose to a juicy breakfast on the balcony of their seaside villa, on the cliffs above the new settlement of Lidion (not to be confused with the capital of Alyinen in the West, of the same name, before its fall).

"Would you like to kill your father then?" Asked Naegeli.

"Hm. Rather not," replied Raedym. "Might not look good for me when I ascend."

Naegeli agreed, and said that it would be best to have a palace guard do the deed late in the night, away from watchful eyes. But she also said that such an execution would take away all sense of enjoyment. And so she killed her husband herself, by bathing him in thick tar harvested from the lands to the near east of Angelon Othim.

Eventually though, Naegeli herself came to the end of all ends. In her revelry and love of making men, she had one night brought in a number of wermen so as to be truly worthy of mention. 87 were brought in all at once, to show their affection to the king in raw and primitive fashion. Such a night it was, with 88 bodies roaring in passion, with such worship thrust upon one seen as divine— Naegeli handled all this rather fine. She sustained no hurt, but scratches and cuts were given to all her 87 suitors that night, all a royal touch of grace.

But when the night grew long and even the strongest of men makers grew tired, at last they came to sleep. And the 87 wermen lie on top of the glorious King Naegeli, who— though immensely powerful— had but the average body of a man nonetheless. And so she suffocated that night, unable to breathe as she slept under the weight of 87.

Her funeral was attended by all the kingdom in that sad year of 2016, even from the farthest pockets of civilization. If the recorded figures are to be believed, then no monarch has ever since come remotely close to garnering the funeral numbers as that of Naegeli. She was beloved to no end, and her tragic death at the small age of 44 was deeply lamented. At least, it could be said that she died in a state of joy, with 87 of her subjects worshiping her perfection, and all of their skins touching, to make the worship pure.

On Raedym

In 2016, at the fresh age of twenty, Raedym the First ascended to his throne, shining as a symbol of health and virtue. All knew that this face would watch over them, smiling, for an age yet to come— surely this young king would outlive his young mother and the lot of them, reigning perhaps until the end of the century.

It was not to be. Few kings of the world have had such swift departures after gaining the throne, and even fewer who were so young. Perhaps none so tragic. But gorgeous Raedym reigned even less than three years in all, succumbing to an illness of the leg at the age of twenty-two.

He traveled far to the East in Dikenia, where he sought to resolve the crises transpiring there. For, years earlier, his mother King Naegeli in her travels had traversed those sprawling lands. She introduced the tribes to the notion of monarchy, and how one especially zealous and influential individual might command a group of thousands, and not just hundreds. The local chieftains nodded to themselves, all of them thinking they knew exactly what Naegeli spoke of, and so they all believed themselves to be zealous and influential, worthy of commanding thousands. And so it was that the entire land was engulfed in war.

When Raedym arrived in Dikenia in 2017, he found a nation that was no nation at all. He was shocked to learn that the climate truly was as dangerous as he had been forewarned, and everywhere he stepped, he snapped his head in all directions to ensure a stone was not hurling towards him.

Little by little, the greatest warlords of Dikenia came to seek an audience with Raedym, and let it be known that they would honor his decision, and his decision alone, for who would rule over their kingdom. Raedym sat in silent council for some days, then gathered all the contesters to a great council at Dokkum, the settlement overlooking the ocean that had long entranced many generations.

The suspense that day was terrible, as Raedym questioned the Dikenian warlords on their prospects as ruler, and bade them all to remain with their hands at their sides, not to kill their neighbors. At last Raedym tossed up his hand, and muttered, "It shall be Cithundin." And so it was that Cithundin the First become the opening king in the royal chapter of Dikenian history.

Raedym never stated outright why he chose Cithundin to lord over his fellow tribes of Dikenia, but contemporary chroniclers all seemed to be in agreement. It was because Cithundin had the most well-crafted face, according to the standards of the Angelons, and he also spoke a great deal of Ferokian. So where he may not have been the strongest choice in terms of sheer ability, he was a king with which Raedym could at least comprehend and relate.

Upon the journey to Angelon, Raedym rode alongside his sister Naemela, and heard nothing but foul talk. For she had learned that their mother had intended to grant her a kingdom in the same manner as Raekal, but had backed out after hearing the counsel of her advisors. "It is not just!" Complained Naemela. "There is more than enough land for the third-born of Naegeli to share in the spoils!" And to bring his sister's mouth to a close, Raedym granted her a kingdom then and there.

"I will call it Lycema," spoke the suddenly placated Naemela, "For it will truly be a place ruled by those with grand tits. Always will our kings be women, to amend for the practice elsewhere, where we are seen as a last resort."

The next two years of Raedym's rule were spent primarily in the establishment of churches, for the lands had fallen out of religion vastly since the days of Marc Vicar and the obliteration of Nephinarthos. Even then, religion consisted of nothing more than a series of legends and fables, to be mulled upon when bored. But Raedym south to hearken back to the ancient voices of the Fourth Age, seeking to worship the gods as they did in the Golden Age of Nephinarthos.

Temples were then erected— not slabs of wooden hut— but glorious, grand feats of architecture that towered above the dwellings of man, and the finest jewels were interlaced in their masonry. Books were compiled, by the most fluid and cohesive writers to be found in the kingdom. These books purported themselves to be thousands of years old, but only recently rediscovered, and ought to be adhered to with the highest of reverence.

The Books of Raedym, then, ushered in a new era for the Angelons: one which consisted of daily visits to the temple, numerous offerings and sacraments, and near constant praise of the household gods which were assigned by royal ministers. In ways, this greatly beneficial to the Kingdom of Angelon, for morality ascended to new heights, but the sanity of her citizens suffered unbearably.

In 2019, Raedym sailed to the Three Islands of Cathuma, where he met with the Grand Priest on business of negotiating an agreed creed between them. His travels to the Island of Pyertis and subsequent meeting with Aggasiz belong to a host of other tales, so it will suffice to say that here, Raedym's left shin was battered in and filled with a poison, one which grew black and green. He returned to Angelon Othim in a miserable state, and there maggots began to poke their heads out of his shin, and grow in size. Within a week they were inches thick, and wiggling in the air, though still planted in the bone. Upon killing the maggots, their venomous secretions crept up Raedym's leg and to the rest of his body, death coming quite quickly.

On Wilderfrant and the Subsequent Four

Wilderfrant the First was raised primarily by his aunt, Naemela, King of Lycema and sister to Raedym I, as he was only a small child when his father died unceremoniously.

To speak swiftly on his many notable achievements, King Wilderfrant I reset the kingdom's currency, codified the national language, created a ministry of advisors to assist in the administration of the realm, and came to define the King's Law as a cornerstone for consistent justice, surpassing the state of affairs in previous reigns where the king would deal out justice on a whim.

It is perhaps consistency that Wilderfrant valued above all else. In all newly recorded instances of injustice, he decided, the proper course of action would be set down in writing to serve as precedent should a similar injustice ever again be committed. The verdicts aimed to be beneficial to those who had been wronged, with compensation deriving from the offender if at all possible. In this way, sentences of execution were often shunned in favor of an outcome where the perpetrator become subservient to the offended party. And in cases of further investigation, if the offended party was proven to be fraudulent in their charge, they would then be at risk of losing two and one half limbs. If fraudulent parties had not two and one half limbs to give, their nose would be cut off instead. But I was never one for speak of the law so I will not attempt to regurgitate further things I have read elsewhere concerning the topic. I am tired and it will most probably come across as mangled upon the page, so let us move on.

For all his love of consistency, Wilderfrant did not however hold consistency with women. He might have called it a certain kind of consistency— a consistency where he consistently harbored new lovers and dealt away with them as they grew aged by a matter of days. An astute reader might point out that he was merely following the habits of his grandmother King Naegeli, who had had her way with wermen just as often, even using them to impregnate her on a whim so that she might put her Stone Chamber to use.

At first, the variety of Wilderfrant's nighttime pleasures had no ill bearing. For the king was young, and of a fine craft, and the women he chose to invite within his chambers were glad. And glad they remained, for as long as the king was willing to give them undivided heed during their allotted time, thus creating the illusion that the passion was full on both ends. But since, as it were, Wilderfrant felt no real love for any of his evening companions, over the course of years he grew bored, and endeavored to find creative new ways to fulfill himself.

Physicians and philosophers of the intimate arts were brought in from Lucilian, where parties of seven or eight were the norm, and from as far as Wethafurd in Dikenia, where the barbaric tribes had crossed all boundaries into the realm of forbidden pleasure. Mountain men from the Angelocs and the far-off Sashites were eventually imported to the kingdom for another enhanced perspective once the fresh charms were again worn off.

To be perfectly clear, Wilderfrant was partaking in orgies every night. But where he differs from the long list of other promiscuous kings over the years is that he bade his deeds of frisk strictly to the dark hours, and would ensure that he never overslept. For in the day he resumed his position, and held up the mantle of the realm, which of all his priorities in life he held in highest esteem.

On the perfection of the codified Ferokian tongue Wilderfrant toiled the long hours, often times from moonset to moonrise, with aims of making the words and writings of those words simple and impactful. Of all the achievements that he might take credit for, Wilderfrant himself said that his contributions to language were among his finest. For communication, he said, was by that time driven fully by speech, and without a consistent language able to be swiftly understood by all, a mutual understanding of life, the world, and one another was futile. And so he spent years collecting samples of local dialects and sifting through them, reconciling the differences, and creating a master book of the Ferokian Tongue that would from then on stand as the undisputed lexicon for the Kingdom of Angelon. In short, Wilderfrant could not stand the thought of people being needlessly misunderstood. Perhaps this arose from the foreboding that he might one day be so himself.

The choosing of the royal officials was fairly simple, for Wilderfrant could recognize innate talent. But in choosing for himself a personal aid— one who could advise upon matters of internal and external policy, assist in the lengthy linguistic project, and simply be a companion for the long tours of the country— the right choice was not so apparent. For years Wilderfrant shifted around members of his inner council, for it wasn't until the year 2044 that the obvious man arrived in Angelon Othim.

Caverith of Clarfinell caught the attention of King Wilderfrant by the simple virtue that he was the only man in the bidding who did not treat the king as a royal figure. When Wilderfrant would complain of his sagging women or of the horrendous sleep he got the night before on his long velvet bed— where others might make an attempt to sympathize— Caverith laughed aloud. And it was this genuine spirit that Wilderfrant was searching for, one who could speak his mind to the king. And one who would not spew nonsense for the sake of being agreeable.

"For of course I have no right to complain of anything," records an ancient dialog between Wilderfrant and Caverith, "I sleep upon the most expensive bed in a hall with the most expensive women and drink from the richest cup the richest wine. That none of these others laughed in my face to hear me grumble is the true cause for concern."

And so Caverith was brought into Wilderfrant's council, and proved to be of high insight and of the same mind as the king on all issues. Even in the chamber of evening pleasures they were of a similar mind, for their dealings with one another did not stop after the business of the royal court. Together they laughed both in and out of doors, enjoying each other's company even when there was nothing to be gained from it. On Athrallia's Day they would walk, or ride, through pleasant wood, and when the snows would strike their city they would retreat to Nephinarthos on the eastern shores of the Sea.

The thing that men most often remember about Wilderfrant and Caverith is their careful study of copulation and the subsequent devising of The Nine Orgasms. They discussed and bickered back and forth for years on the true number and nature of The Nine Orgasms, and they eventually concurred— but whatever they were, they are lost to us. Perhaps this is what the pair of them wanted: to let a hundred generations thereafter know that they had indeed discovered the true Nine Orgasms, but not to record them in any fashion. They have certainly inspired a long list of imitators; every culture upon Elaptirius has their own idea of what The Nine Orgasms are. But as to those that Wilderfrant and Caverith decided upon, that secret has gone away with them quietly to the tombs.

Also going away with them quietly to the tombs is the true nature and extent of their relationship. Long have men decried that Wilderfrant and Caverith engaged in their evening pleasures together— as in directly to one another— while an equal part declare that they merely studied the copulations together, each in turn partaking with the numerous women present but never venturing to clash the two forks so to speak.

Whether they did clash the forks or not, it is not for us to say. Whether Wilderfrant felt a passion of fire for his preferred lord is also not for us to declare. While abundantly clear that Wilderfrant found in Caverith a deep relationship that he failed to reap with his woman relations, it is clouded— and indeed irrelevant— whether the king harbored any affectation for his lord. Either way, they were grand companions, and would continue on as such until an inevitable adventure reared its wings.

For in the year 2056, Wilderfrant did for Caverith what Naegeli had done for Raekal and Naemela in granting them Enceloth and Lycema. He granted him a territory of his own to govern, and they called it the Longpis. The biggest difference between the Longpis and Enceloth or Lycema, of course, was that the Longpis actually lay beyond the borders of Angelon. So in granting this land to Caverith, Wilderfrant was not simply handing over a piece of his own kingdom. Rather, he was laying down a pact of conquest, that he would provide the necessary army to march south and subdue what peoples they found in that land.

The Conquest of the Longpis lasted the better part of the year, but it was done without major setback. In those days the southern edge of Angelon was defined by the River Gizle, with but few Angelon explorers ever crossing over. Those who had, had found a docile countryside, with wide stretches of rolling hill, sparsely populated. It was a fair place to be conquered then, both in terms of the character of its geology and its peoples.

An ancient series of forts existed along the Gizle, directly south from the South Tip of the Sea. These forts had over the years slowly grown into a conglomeration of towns known as Gizelia, and when Wilderfrant and Caverith came riding down they found great joy and hospitalities in its homely inns. Caverith, who was more for luxury than his king— who found himself to be comforted anywhere as long as the intent was pure— found the inns to be a bit lacking. "Very well," spoke Wilderfrant over the dim light of a wooden table, "When the lands south of this great river are yours to hold, then you may put all your efforts into the creation of the most lavishing inns and taverns. As for my country, we will hold yet to the simple ways of the past as long as we might, and take pleasure from them."

They crossed over the Gizle on into unknown lands, with nothing but rudimentary charts and writings from a group of explorers who had gone before, in the days of Francil, over a century ago. True enough were claims to the fairness of the land, and by the end of the first day's march they came to another great river, one with a hue far more yellow and tainted than the great blue and silver streams of the Gizle. "Perhaps we've come to the edge of your kingdom already," joked Wilderfrant. But Caverith endeavored to push on, thinking it ridiculous that any ruler worthy of mention would have a territory able to be traversed in a day.

They made course to follow the river without crossing, for in the writings of Francil's explorers they told of words shared with natives, saying that the great yellow river led onwards to the ocean, a sight which Caverith very much longed to see. Even Wilderfrant at this point had not yet cast eyes upon the endless blue, despite now being a 39-year-old monarch. Truly, the great yellow river did lead to the ocean— eventually— but the course was so mangled and twisted that all the men were up in arms.

"Who designed this river?!" Exclaimed one angry soldiers.

"Whoever crafted our world!" Yelled back Wilderfrant, or Caverith. "And it would be a glorious design if only we could see it from far above. As we chart it now for the first time, it appears to take the form of a snake, and so I say we call it the Snaketail River." And so it has been called, ever since.

The Incident of the Dogpit is the last thing I will tell of the first Conquest of the Longpis. Among the barbaric tribes along the Snaketail River, Wilderfrant and Caverith found one that rejoiced in the battling of armored dogs, who were made to fight til death. Wilderfrant approached, any sign of his kingly status removed, and asked how much it would be to buy all the dogs. The Dogpit Lord spit up his nose.

Wilderfrant then inquired as to how many dogs were equal to the life of one of his men. Here, the Dogpit Lord spit into Wilderfrant's ears, and said that sixty men would get him one dog. Wilderfrant gave the Dogpit Lord one more chance, and with diplomacy stated: "I will leave you my entire host of one hundred men, to replace your dogs, and you may fight them to the death. But then I will take all of your dogs as payment."

To this proposal, the Dogpit Lord opened Wilderfrant's mouth and spat in it two hundred times, twice for each of the proposed men. After enduring this, Wilderfrant muttered a cynical remark to himself, and ordered a charge of cavalry. All in this Dogpit Tribe were gathered by force, and made to dig a soggy pit in the earth, which they were all then cast into and buried alive. The dogs were set free.

There was much laughter between Wilderfrant and Caverith as they returned to Angelon, but all the other men were sour because their king had proposed trading their lives for the possession of dogs. This was just the beginning of Glorious Wilderfrant's problems, for her troubles would soon begin to bloom.

Soon after the Conquest of the Longpis, Wilderfrant began to court the members of his own inner circle. These were not mere admirers who would have given anything for a night with the king. These were haughty individuals with their own ideas as to their worth, and each began to feel as if the king's affections should go wholly towards their own bodies. They cried out at end to the king's promiscuous ways.

Soon doubt began to grow in all other areas of Wilderfrant's rule, to no good purpose. The jealous lovers of the king planted these seeds of doubt, and spread them to all winds, decrying Wilderfrant as one who was unable to rule justly. The folk of Angelon at this time were now grown tired of subservience, and these ideas of governance liberty took root in their minds, and they were all for a time fiercely independent, and sure of their own intelligence.

"We are able folk, and well would we govern ourselves!" Was the cry heard from the streets. And they brought forth havoc upon the lords and ministers of justice.

In this way, Wilderfrant became the first king to be ousted from his throne while at the same time being given the chance to live out the rest of his life. Reluctantly, he sought refuge in the Land of the Longpis, which was only just beginning to thrive under his friend Caverith.

"Isn't this a thing of irony," smirked Caverith upon his throne, which he fashioned in the shape of a tongue. "You the great King of Angelon take this land by force and give it to me, but now it is you who are without land. Well, I will not forget the honor by which I hold my throne. You are always welcome here." And they embraced. And may or may not have made men after.

But far up in Angelon, those who had never before dreamed of ruling now found themselves with the reigns of governance.

And the people suffered greatly.

For all were now fighting for their own selfish interest, and were unable to bring any others under their own dominion. The stable tree of law and justice were broken, as factions spilt apart to form new factions, increasing by the day, and physical combat was the only way to settle an argument. Theft occurred daily, and the laws of Wilderfrant thrown out. In every way it was a hard time for those who endeavored to make good and pleasant deeds.

Then, on a cold day in Uanethis, Wilderfrant went for a walk through snow in the white woods of Frawlin, where he and Caverith many times rode. He had returned quietly in the waning years of his life, for he was no longer hunted, and he had missed the fair places of his youth. He lamented the misery that shook across his land, but could not help but to laugh at their plight. For he had served them well, and ushered in many great things that had not yet been seen in that corner of the world. And then by their own hand did they tear him from his home, to the thought that they could do better.

Here in the woods a host of young liberators bowed before the man of old age, holding out their hands and begging Wilderfrant to draw their blood as a sign of their allegiance.

"I know not," spoke Wilderfrant. "It was liberators that took from me my home."

"We are now liberators of a different kind," spoke their young leader, her eyes letting the big tears fall. "We seek to be liberators of the liberators, who have liberated us into darkness."

And so the king returned to his throne in the year 2077, to right the wrongs that had been done in his absence. Though past the age of 80, he acted as a young man with purpose, and brought his favorite son near to him upon his bed of death "I realize well that your name is Phobe, but you might choose another, son. For I would not live to see a King Phobe rule over this land. But, as it were that my reign was significantly less than what it ought to have been, perhaps take my name, so that I might fulfill those long years in your life, where I could not in my own."

And Phobe concurred, taking his father's name for the rest of his days. And the custom would be continue, to an aggravating extent, one that the original Wilderfrant surely would not have foreseen.

To speak briefly on the next lot of kings, who we have scant writings of:

Wilderfrant II married off nine of his horses to children (not his own children, but children that he conscientiously picked) and then formed his own Horse Society, the gates of which are still adhered to in Lucilian.

Wilderfrant III invited all the Nephinarthins who had escaped the wrath of Marc Vicar back to their homeland and promised that the Kingdom of Angelon would forevermore be a sworn protector of all the cities round the Sea, thus initiating the Nephinarthin Alliance in 2111.

Wilderfrant IV was a great master of arches, and built what was then the tallest building in the known world: The Watchtower of Gizelia. He also had a series of bridges constructed nearby on the Gizle, opening up trade routes and exploration into the region that would become Dunland.

Wilderfrant V commanded that all vendors of food and drink guarantee their output to be good, for which his people praised him.

And here we come to Wilderfrant VI, who for the longest of times was thought to be but another Penflath. In the first 61 years of his kingship, nothing was written of him. Or so we are led to believe. In truth, there may have been some semblance of recorded deed regarding the sixth Wilderfrant, but they were all most likely destroyed by a great enemy. For, rising in the Southeast, an adversary was ascending.

Tidings to Angelon Othim came in 2275 of an unstoppable darkness, writhing out of the twisted labyrinths of Ansila Siroth, and finding its way ever north, beginning towards the west. Wilderfrant VI, or the Old King as he was now called— for he too had named his son Wilderfrant— thought little of these warnings. But by the council of his son the Young King he was persuaded to ride south, and there he faced the true extent of rising horror.

Here we must diverge, before telling of the infamous WAR OF HAEGOS, for the telling of the pre-eminent mythology of Denderrin Othim— where Kezhil laid the stones for a time when Caldar would walk among men, and Melizar thereafter — which has up til now been postponed, must now be told.

Part Three

Lords of Ancient Places

On Tiluma and Gelseth

Few stop to ponder how the sun and the stars and the moons gained their place in the heavens. Many look up and spot the celestial spheres well enough, seeing them as custom, without viewing them as wonder. Indeed, in my day many have come to disregard the legends which I am about to relate as mere folly and farce.

To begin, allow me to set the stage by declaring that the land we rest upon is not the first that was made in Cotialla. According to the tales herein, relating to the ancient religious following called the Tilumathen, all the world we inhabit— or rather did for eleven ages until all but recently— can be referred to as Overlind. And Overlind, then, rests above the Realm of Margon, that being the supreme paradise found far under ground, where the Ancient Lords resided long ago.

Margon was said to be a perfected vision of creation, which existed for near an eternity before all the works of Overlind, and has never before been glimpsed by any of our kind, unless we are to believe the words of the great epic CLARFONATH. In which case, one mortal man has glimpsed Margon, and only then right before it was reportedly flooded. But for the rest of us who don't happen to be Clarfon Both, we can have no true knowledge on the reality of Margon, for that was always its purpose— to remain forever hidden from the eyes of those born above.

Whether or not the Realm of Margon still lies far beneath our feet, the Tilumathen have grown silent, for the matter has become irrelevant to Passian-kind. There was never a way to reach this sacred land, and any word coming up from it ceased long ages ago, and therefore it is possible that Margon was never a tangible place at all. But let us assume that it was, for several things more remarkable have transpired over the years.

Now then, Tiluma was the High Lord of Margon, stationed above all others in beauty, grace, and power. He was not the creator of Margon, as is made clear by all— the identity of the first creator has been said to be concealed deliberately— but he was given his rank of High Lord directly by will of that creator. And with his grand majesty, Tiluma reigned over towers of shining glass, under a domed roof of colored stone stretching on into eternity. For there was yet no sky in Margon, and hence no fear of the elements— all was perpetually in peace, with the cities resting between lower ground and upper, in no need of light for their bodies were made of it pure.

Of the lives of the Margonathi we know little; indeed we know the names of only three. We would know none at all if it were not for Gelseth, who diverted the course of history— or enabled history to begin, as some say. For Gelseth, although identical to his Margonathi brethren in beauty and grace, had something that was not intended of him: desire. And with his desire, Gelseth wished to be loved in the manner of Tiluma. For at all times Tiluma was worshipped by all of Margon, and as Tiluma orchestrated the perfect music, all eyes were forever on him.

The song was always the same. There was one song, and it was played to perfection.

For Tiluma would have no other. He was placed as perfect lord, amidst perfect land, by perfect creator, and therefore there was no reason to sing anything but that which he knew to be perfection. And so the Margonathi sang in unison, in harmony, in reverence. But never astray.

And Gelseth held deep thoughts. They deepened, as ages passed but went nowhere, and at last he bowed before Tiluma in the shining tower of his splendor, and asked if he might sing on his own. Impossible, was Tiluma's reply. To rise above and apart from his own kind, when he was clearly not the Lord chosen by the Creator. He would mar the perfection of existence. He was warned extensively to abide.

And abide Gelseth did, for many more passes of peaceful time. But the Song That Was Sung began to grow on him in different ways, and Gelseth could feel it changing. Always the orchestration of Tiluma made the song soft and slow, with a sweetness of innocence of a grandeur of love and adoration. But in his deepening thought, Gelseth could feel the song gripping him, tightly it would seem, and even thrashing him about.

At last Gelseth could hold the breaking tide no longer. As the Choir of Margon sang the Song That Was Sung for Tiluma, soft and slow, so Gelseth broke pace. He sang loud and high above the others' pitch, and the rhythm sped. The Margonathi are said to have been split— many feeling Gelseth's new rendition to be abhorrent, but many finding it to be of a new elation. And this was what brought fear into Tiluma's mind.

Or not fear— as the Tilumathen say to this day— for Tiluma has no fear in his endless power. What was it he felt then, at the base of his sentience? It is said he turned immediately to anger, but is not the base of all anger fear, even for the gods?

The Tilumathen proclaim the High Lord's anger was noble and his swift response for the good of all, who would have been led astray into darkness and imperfection by the foul song of Gelseth. For Tiluma, it is said, could see into Gelseth's mind. And he saw, in this moment of rebellion, a mind set on the dismantling of Margon, of claiming lordship for himself, and of bringing all to ruin. And so, in the interest of all the perfection in his midst, Tiluma rid Margon of its dark speck, and bid him to return never— to suffer an eternal sentence of pain which would be known to all, and seen by all until the dying days of creation, and by which his name would become synonymous with all that is crooked and wrong, ridiculed by every living thing.

Gelseth was placed on the First Sun. Newly created by Tiluma specially for this torment, the roof of Margon was cracked and many were the awe as the violet void was glimpsed for the first time. And in this void, Tiluma sent up a burning sphere, to which he fastened Gelseth with an ever-tightening chain of worm-flesh.

The Margonathi felt a darkness lash through them as suddenly — without warning, amidst their perfection— they now beheld one of their own blacken and crisp, his beautiful form forever ruined, all within moments. And as he rose, tied to the growing sphere of flame, black grew to black, and farther black than that— a new definition of black at every snap for beings that had never known any absence of light. And though Gelseth was brought to this impossible shade within a matter of seconds, Tiluma swore that his body would continue to grow blacker and blacker until the end of time, as the flames of his host would only intensify. And thus no black of night nor any element found upon our earth can begin to compare to the absence of light in Gelseth today, who has now been imprisoned on the First Sun for at least ten thousand years.

The Margonathi were surely frightened, perhaps even overwrought with hopelessness, after witnessing the damnation of Gelseth upon the Sun. But such was the aim of Tiluma. For knowing well that no being of Margon could match him in power, he had effectively crushed all notion of desire that Gelseth may have bred within them. For who now would stand for any but the will of Tiluma, after seeing the unspeakable fate that awaited those who would challenge him?

On Kezhil

Generations went by, although they could not be called generations. Centuries passed, though they could not be called centuries. For in the Under Realm of Margon time moves altogether differently than on the surface, and these events all occurred well before the start of the Earthly Beings. But some amount of a passing swept over the Margonathi, enough for many to forget all memories of the Casting of Gelseth.

Here enters Kezhil, one who would at a later time become synonymous with all evil and horror, wrongdoing and malice. But all who speak of the days before Trosis concur that Kezhil was, at this time, both curious and studious. He organized a great hall of learning, and bid for all Margonathi to know the order of things— not so that they might rule in place of

Tiluma, as has been incorrectly gestured by ill-informed Tilamathens— but so they would better enshrine themselves in the glory of creation.

While gathering tales and ancient memory, Kezhil the Margonathi heard from one just as ancient as Tiluma, on the subject of the Casting of Gelseth. And Kezhil grew scared in his heart, as if all the world he knew were a lie. For if this were true, and if Tiluma the Almighty truly had cast away one with such ease and on a moment's whim, then all existence within the bounds of sight were doomed to be ruled by fear forever.

And with this thought brewing in his mind, Kezhil turned from Tiluma.

Tiluma was now grown old. And one might ask how one who is all-powerful and charged with the lording over all the realm could be made to grow old— and it is a just question. For Tiluma, by design, was not meant to age while in the confines of this creation. But all beings possess the power of mind in this world, and the mind is the principle driver of what we call age. So although he would never die, still Tiluma was grey at this time, and walked slow without spring, and felt a disenchantment with all his perfection. And so it was that Kezhil was able to walk behind closed doors and evade the detection of Almighty Tiluma.

For Kezhil was now building a rebellion, full and true, that which Gelseth might one day have come to realize had he not been instantaneously cast into torment (not to make conjecture upon Gelseth— who quite probably was only trying to introduce new music into the Realm of Margon). But now Kezhil's aim was to right the wrongs of that day, for he viewed the Casting of Gelseth as a heinous overstep of power on Tiluma's part.

Many of the Margonathi agreed with Kezhil. Some were old and had been present to witnesses the horrors that befell Gelseth, but were always without hope in rising, for fear that they would face the same fate. Yet many of these same Margonathi knew Kezhil's rebellion to be equally hopeless, for none could stand tall in the face of Tiluma, no matter the number. And so Kezhil and his followers would bind these Margonathi that did not fully pledge allegiance, knowing well that they would inform Tiluma of their treason if kept free.

And so this building of resistance held for some time, with Tiluma hardly knowing the better. But one day, a Margonathi who had pledged herself to Kezhil's cause betrayed Kezhil, and informed Tiluma of the treachery that was brewing behind his neck. Tiluma laughed, and thought he might revel more in this than he had with Gelseth. And so he allowed Kezhil to continue gaining forces, and would only come to meet him when all the realm had been approached.

Once Kezhil's following had become truly grand, then it would have seemed ridiculous not to join. For if— as many supposed — Tiluma could not sense treachery at his doorstep and squash the rebellion at once, then he must truly have no power left in his being. When the vastness of Margon seemed to side with Kezhil, and yet Tiluma remained silent, then it became abundantly clear that Kezhil would soon be victor and lord of the land, and so it would be foolish to remain loyal to Tiluma. They had nearly all of them been persuaded, not by faith in Kezhil, but by faith that Tiluma had truly grown into nothing but an old being, unable to summon the powers that he once had. For in truth it had been long since Tiluma presented any show of strength, and he looked old and withered in the eyes of the beautiful Margonathi. This is how nearly all the beings of that age came to be in the host of Kezhil, rising up against the god whom all praised in unceasing loyalty for eternities before. For many the choice was blind, and out of fear, or out of certain knowledge that he would prevail.

At last came the day when all of Margon had chosen their lot. Tiluma sat resting in his bed of waters, his long white beards drifting through air. And Kezhil marched upon the gates of his palace, with almost all the host of Margon marching behind him. It is said that of all those who lived on that day, 273 out of every 274 were counted in the Force of Kezhil. Raging on Tiluma's walls they all screamed out abhorrent curses, believing Tiluma to be a helpless elder of bygone days. They desecrated his waters and tore his fabrics, demanding justice for Gelseth and accusing him of tyranny, saying that all his existence was a mar upon Margon— a land that would have been truly perfect had it not been for him.

And at last Tiluma rose, a shining tear falling slow from his face. "How has it come to this?" He asked himself. And as the voices of rebellion rose ever louder, he at last silenced them, so that they would listen.

"I am the lord of this place," said Tiluma, softly. Looking up and around, he made contact with billions of his once-followers all within a drop. He, closing his eyes, resumed "I was made so by the perfect creator, whose name I alone will know until we come to a new place. For this one has shown itself to be evil. And of a burning impurity of which it will now never be rid. Why, Kezhil? Did you really think you could take this land for yourself?"

Kezhil, if he could, would have surely rejected this accusation and stated to the last his one desire for Gelseth's resurrection, but he— like all in his army— were froze.

"You seek justice for Gelseth," continued Tiluma, his beard floating off and his grey turning to gold, "Yet you do so by walking the same path that led to his banishment. It is only sensical that those who walk the same path will eventually come upon the same end."

And Tiluma set them all ablaze.

And just as had been done with Gelseth, a new flaming sphere was formed from Tiluma's hand, and rising up towards the roof of Margon it grew large— ever larger, for this Sun was of need to imprison billions— and forever hot.

This was the Second Sun, and for the reason just stated it rests far superior to its predecessor in our daytime sky. For upon it are held the billions of souls that dared to rise against Tiluma in Margon, and believed for a brief moment in time the words of what could be in a world without Tiluma— the words of Kezhil.

On Caldar

Unlike Kezhil, who was not completely abhorrent in nature—his sole downfall being the choice to rebel against Tiluma, on debatably noble terms— Caldar would grow to become a fully relentless lord of darkness. All things that are dark in this world have become so by his hand, and it is said that it he who realized the potency of true evil out of the fragments devised by Gelseth and Kezhil.

And yet, at first it was not so. At first he was a Starling, bright and fair like all the rest, though perhaps in not all ways the same, which has proven to the detriment of all.

Now it was that Starlings came about in the First Age of Overlind, which was created shortly after the Casting of Kezhil, for there was now a large hole in the top of Margon, and those Margonathi still in the service of Tiluma climbed up and began to create the world as we knew it, on the upper side of Margon's roof.

On the nature of how the Margonathi came to create Overlind and all the lands herein, I am not at liberty to say. Nor would it fit in with this tale of histories. I will simply say that here Tiluma is said to have played the part of creator, in giving life to the Primordial Starlings and perhaps the first of the Passians as well, though that much is in doubt. For after creating the Primordial Starlings, Tiluma craved a reward for his long doings, and took one of his creations— the most beautiful b y all standards— and made for her to be his wife. This Primordial Starling was Athrallia, now elevated to High Goddess of Margon. But before descending down into their eternal kingdom, Athrallia was granted her wish to create something living for herself, and so the meticulous crafting that has gone into the making of our bizarre species is said to be the doing of Athrallia. Yes, the same Athrallia whose sacred piss served as the catalyst for the CLARFONATH.

Now we will take a leap to the birth of Caldar. In those days, the Starlings took rest at the rising of the suns and did not wake until the skies once again grew dark. Then they would walk in starlight, themselves emitting soft light, drifting slowly through peaceful wood. On a heavenly night such as this Caldar rose out of watery springs fashioned by Tiluma, as did all the Primordial Starlings, in the southwest corner of the Far End Green Woods, which were called Gwidenarsa, just north of the Great Grey.

Here he was reared in the same fashion as all his kin, though in the year of his rising there were no other Starlings that followed. Neither then nor in the next season, nor the next. And so Caldar was alone throughout the greater part of his growing, with elder Starlings and utterly unaware of the nature of his young counterparts.

Now, but few short years after the birth of Caldar, rose one whose name would also thunder across time. She was Alyin, and Alyin was an exceptionally stunning creature, a creation of sublime fortitude in the eyes of Tiluma, who is said to have held a personal stake in her making. She rose in a patch of many others, and while they all admired her beyond telling— for she was undoubtedly the most beautiful of them all and would be said so for all of foreseeable time— they did not pursue her. No one would claim her, no one wanted her for their own. For how could such perfection rightly be contained in the grip of one singular being? How could the precious glimmering gems found on her ankles— which were found on all Starlings but none to this level of perfection— be held by any so unworthy?

And so all the Starlings of Gwidenarsa spoke with her, and walked with her, and lay in fine gardens with her, on the swinging beds between the trees, without any thought of possession. It was as natural for them, these beautiful conversings, as taking a sip from their endless fountains. But Caldar, though one of their own, could find no easy way to approach her.

And yet he craved for her. Not in the evil ways of men who have since tainted the playful joys of loves, for evil did not yet exist in the woods of Gwidenarsa. Evil was far out of the minds of all, and it could not be conceived— even by the one who was to introduce it into the world and champion its meaning until this very day. Strange as it may sound, Caldar desired Alyin in the most simplistically innocent way imaginable.

He would lurk in the trees and stare out at her, but only for lack of the courage to approach her. Did he realize she could sense his eyes resting upon her neck? Perhaps, and perhaps this deluded Starling thought his gaze would be enough to communicate his desire to the precious Alyin. But Alyin did not understand— none of the other Starlings acted this way towards her, and certainly none of them had any form of hesitation in speaking to her. Then she could only assume that this Caldar who peered at her through woods was of ill intent, even though such a thing had never been thought of in all the world, and she was not in comfort.

Alyin spoke of this to the other Starlings, and they failed to comprehend her meaning. How could she feel a sense of unease when all of Gwidenarsa was made as it should be, with all their wants and needs provided by the will of Tiluma? Yet Alyin spoke more of this "unease" and of a certain "dread" that fingered her every time Caldar was near.

Years turned in the celestial forest, and Caldar continued to dream of the heavenly Alyin. He had not the slightest fear of Alyin's discomfort, for such things were as yet foreign to him as well. He dreamed only of fulfilling every one of her desires, to be a sort of servant to her as she walked through wood and river, lifting her white cloak as she treaded the softened trails and cleansing her feet thereafter. He wished most of all to hear the sound of her voice responding to words that he himself spoke, and to hold those words in his mind as an affirmation of the true goodness of Tiluma's creation. Such things would have been enough for the small mind of that long gone Caldar, a simple Starling in the dayless wood.

But years of planning his words did not bring gladness. For the time had welled in Alyin, who now felt a horror wrench upon her every time she glimpsed Caldar from the other side of the trees. She even thought she saw him stealing looks at her, even when he wasn't there at all. So when Caldar at last emerged from his place in the shadows, to stand before her in open clearing, Alyin recoiled. She kept vigilant watch at all times that she might never be cornered by him.

In the pure mind of an ancient Starling in those woods of Gwidenarsa, the only thing to do in the hour of need was to seek the counsel of Tiluma. And so Caldar did what any other would have done in his situation, though this circumstance was unlike any other that would ever be in that realm. He called upon Tiluma to speak.

For a full passage of seasons Caldar prayed, beckoning his good lord Tiluma. But he never answered. From the beginning, instead there was a whisper in the willows, one who called himself Kezhil. But Caldar knew well the Doom of Kezhil— of his eternal damnation upon the Second Sun— sharing twin fate with Gelseth. He refused to answer.

But upon the passing of more seasons, Caldar began to lose hope. Tiluma would not answer, whereas the voice of Kezhil would flow forth every time. At first a whisper, it grew into a clear ringing, no longer from the trees but coming from inside Caldar's own heart.

He, Kezhil, spoke in dark riddles, telling Caldar of all that he sought to gain through the Pursuit of Alyin.

"There are more than just words to be had with her, Caldar. Her body is something to be craved even more so. And ravished."

"Ravished?" Replied Caldar, in need of explanation. Here, the voice of Kezhil filled the mind of Caldar with heinous thoughts of violation, of grabbing hold of things by force and subduing all to his own will, and here feelings of power— power beyond limit— must've first ran across Caldar's darkening soul.

For he did desire Alyin in the flesh. And he felt certain as he gazed across his fellow Starlings that they all did as well, they just hadn't been awakened to it yet. And so on the first day of Serallia, Caldar summoned the Starlings of Gwidenarsa to a council, where he interrogated his fellow beings on their desires concerning Alyin.

The pure answers rung out. Not a word of skin, nor of partaking in that which Alyin would not suggest herself. "What are you then," posed Caldar, "Slaves to one of your own? That you would have her command you in all ways, but you would not dare move her through your own wills? Why do we not embrace the desires within, when every one of hers is made real?"

And the Starlings now saw what Alyin forebode. They revealed to Caldar her discomfort, and bade him to exile. Here Caldar was stricken mad, for he never realized the true extent of Alyin's disdain towards him. He was in denial, for how could she truly detest anything in a world where nothing was to be detested? But somehow it had sprung, and now the voice of Kezhil rung louder in his head that pain had been brought into the world for him to champion.

So Caldar fled Gwidenarsa, but not before snatching Alyin from her bed and hiding her in the belly of a great tree, which he struck and hallowed out after fashioning the first axe in all of Elaptirius— indeed the first of any sharp tool ever fashioned from stone. And because of its high effect in cutting out the back of the tree, Caldar continued to use it.

He brought his stone down upon the body of Alyin, for so long the desire of all his dreams. His hands would run across her for long after, but the first to ravage her was the stone. And here such blood was shed that set into motion all the wars of the coming ages, and all the sins of passion that would stain across our history.

The Starlings of Gwidenarsa pursued Caldar to his hollowed tree, but Caldar murdered all who approached. His mind was growing fast to the ways of treachery, and all the ways of defeating an opponent. Though the Starlings were not much to bring down, having never encountered malice before in their existence. So Caldar smote them easily.

Taking and torturing his fellow beings, he managed to convert several to his will, while many others perished at his hands. With his new servants, he returned to Gwidenarsa and sacked the forest, bringing the First Flame to Overlind, which he discovered through the voice of Kezhil. Amidst the blaze, Caldar recovered the great Starling artifacts— gems and stones and staffs— that he would manipulate to new purposes, bringing his power to an even greater extent.

And after wandering for what must have been centuries upon the Western plains, Caldar settled in Darkwood, in the land we now call Neutralia, near the waning of the First Age. Here he would remain for thousands of years, everyday growing more evil and expanding his heinous dominion over his expanded following.

To occupy his time most predominantly, Caldar set to work constructing new forms of life in the pools below the Falls of Darkwood, in little caverns where he would use his tools to cross beast with beast. The horse is a creature that came from this process, and it may be that this animal is the one truly great thing that has come out of Caldar's existence. Though for a long stretch of time, horses would only be employed for dark purposes, such as his evil steed Lontik, and to this day our enemies are aided by sweeping rows of steed that perhaps it would have been better had the species never been brought to life at all.

Into the Second Age, mortal Passians began to find their way into Darkwood, after wandering far from their first home devised by Athrallia in the Garden of Trosis. Darkwood was not a natural choice for roaming peoples without home, but their coming to this deep place of high evil can be explained through Caldar's methods of treachery. For he would alight the paths of men with softened glows, inviting them with warmth and promises of easy rest amidst a place both soothing and harmonious.

He was the Great Whisperer, passing even Kezhil in his skill with quiet words to bend hearts to his will. For though now a dark lord of cruelty, he was still Starling by form and retained all their great powers of transmission through clear air. When he had tempted men far along the falsely lighted path, the lights went out— never to return, for those within range of Caldar were struck blind. Sight could be restored but only by his grace, and he would only permit things to be seen by his captured beings that which he saw fit. These unfortunate peoples were called the Desiroth, and they would be forced to reproduce at alarming rates with any whom Caldar chose, breeding an army that would stretch down from the Second Age to the Fifth.

Perhaps it was his ill-disputed mastery of enchantment, or a genuine effectiveness as a master, but in those days none who entered the service of Caldar ever left. Rebellions were unheard of; loyalty was full-fold. Which may be a testament to some sort of astonishing quality on the dark lord's behalf. Or perhaps simply to his vast power, so terrible that any opposition from within would be useless in the blinded eyes of his Desiroth. For indeed there was a purpose to this apparent madness of endless cruelty. Caldar one day intended to roam out of Darkwood, back into the West, and take control of all the lands from Rocksend to the Sestarions.

The time to act came towards the close of the Third Age, when Passians had established themselves far and wide across modern-day Stonearch. And so Caldar sent forth Desiroth spies to bring back tidings from every civilized place stretching out from Darkwood to the West and northwest (he would not yet attempt the Eastern Lands of Elaptirius, for the tall and rocky peaks of the Sashites did not bode well amongst his armies).

The Desiroth spread all about the incredibly varied landscapes, finding each village to be of different stock and all speaking in different tongues. They tried their best to organize their findings on parchment, since Caldar had commanded them to bring back maps and knowledge of the areas at his doorstep, but the Desiroth could do nothing more than to separate the peoples they found into four groups of vaguely similar cultures, though their divisions were blurred.

Rushing back to Darkwood, they informed the curious Caldar, who then provided the four divisions of the land with the names Gandrypool, Glitharog, Garrigal, and Gwidenarsa. They reported that a central authority was nonexistent across all lands, with the peoples being mere farmers and their knowledge of weapons bare. The only hint of an army to be found was the ancient Riverguard, a host of Passians who guarded the west side of the Urf, to keep out the fell beasts that would on occasion roam out of Darkwood. It was here then, that Caldar would choose to strike hardest and most swiftly.

The Crossing of Caldar occurred upon the Upper Urf, between the Glimmer Lake and Salar. So horrible was that night to behold, that even from an age where hardly a tale survives, it has come down to us from countless fronts. All who were part of it must've related it to their children as soon as they could listen, and never did it fail to be passed down. It is indeed one of the greatest accounts of any event we have across this wide land.

It happened late in the night, on an especially black night, when starlight was shunned by heavy cloud. Yet the dark lord and his Desiroth did not pass by unopposed. Hundreds of men of the Riverguard had gathered in the narrow crossing, where the clear waters only came about knee-high, before rippling down a small bout of rapids. They had heard Caldar's coming with their own ears, for the Desiroth and beasts of the trees carried along ugly chants of war and torment as they made their way out of Darkwood.

Now then, ancient men of the Riverguard held the western shore of the Urf, some of them wading in the calm river, looking up at the wooded hill to the east. Mutilated men of the Desiroth began streaming down, quietly at first, with hissing cackles of wicked pleasure and anticipation as they leaped down slopes and hid themselves behind trees. This was the night they had waited for, all the days of their long anguished lives, and for some, perhaps the only night that might ever bring them any semblance of joy.

The Riverguard did not wait for the Desiroth to cross. With their rudimentary bows they fired flint arrows at the trees where the enemies hid. Cautiously, they sent up axe-wielders to the East Hill to cut down what Desiroth they could, though here Caldar's men had the upper hand and would unexpectedly lash out from their hidings and cast the axe-wielders into the river.

Near the darkest hour of the night, the Captain of the Riverguard at last called up, demanding that the Desiroth move forward so that they might have a fair fight in the river. The Desiroth descended onto the bank, forming a wide line that stretched out of eyesight. They joined swords, of which each of them had two, and walked forward in an unbreakable wave. Here, the Riverguard would have been slaughtered within minutes (and indeed many of them were) but for the coming of reinforcements from the Far End Green Woods: a vibrant force of warriors with four Starlings among the charge. One of these was Alyin, the Primordial who had been the bane of Caldar from his earliest days.

With the help of Alyin and her fellow Starlings, the Desiroth were held at bay, until Caldar himself began to descend the hill. The Riverguard gazed in awe as Caldar marched forward — they had heard his whispers for countless generations but none outside Darkwood had yet gazed upon his form. He was all black now, with a smooth leathery shell of skin akin to a lizard, spotted but yet unexplainably consistent, glimmering even without a light. From all sides, long pale white strands protruded from him, fluttering in terrifying beauty and whisping around his long helmet. The helmet covered the whole of his face, with sharp extensions dropping down to his chest. His mouth was a layered cavern of salivous flaps, each with brownish-white teeth circled on all sides. The mouth lie near the top of the head, while the eyes— slowly swirling clouds of vibrant green— lay below, in the center. Both his eyes and mouth had large lids that could lower over them, and it was this closed appearance that was his resting pose, only opening the eyes and mouth for heinously delicious deeds.

It is said that the archers would freeze in immediate terror, losing all sense of muscle as he approached. And with his foe immobilized Caldar would grab the back of the head and thrust it down into the water, if the force of his hand was not enough to crush the skulls outright. After drowning upwards of fifty men in the shallow stream, the night at last took a turn. For Alyin was seen drifting between pine on the western slope. At first smell of her paradistic aroma, Caldar shed tears that dropped into the water a green luminescence. He then looked up, and at seeing her long eyes, smoothly rounding across into sharp and powerful ends, he found himself defeated. Then and there he commanded all his force to halt, and spoke directly to Alyin. If she would hold council with him, just the two of them, he would send all his own back to Darkwood that night. But Alyin fled.

And so, shamed of his dejected show of weakness, and with two angry armies still knee-deep in water, the fight resumed. Caldar killed all who remained in the river, swiftly, for he wished to follow Alyin before she got too far out of his reach.

But the will of Alyin was strong, and adamant was she never speak to the heinous fiend that had introduced evil into the world. Despite years of fire and torment, with all the kind creatures of the West always on the flee, never knowing peace — still Alyin hid. Even when Caldar made known to her that all his rage would be ended if only she would share words with him. Still she hid.

At last, after years of devastation, Caldar cornered her in Trilsenyamar, on the border of the Chipperin Woods. She was sitting beneath the old stone bridge, and there she sat, with an army of a thousand circled around. Caldar approached and chained her to the bridge, so she would not escape, then ordered his army to depart. Then, in the privacy of wet green wood, at last he and Alyin spoke.

Their words are secret, and belong to only them. But we know from history that they must have come to some sort of agreement, for the plunderings of Caldar came to be only fractional of their potential. What Alyin offered or promised in return for his mercy we can but speculate. But indeed for a great stretch of time, Caldar ceased upon force, disbanded his armies, and wandered the west of the world in a roaming passiveness.

For several generations then Caldar haunted the forests and streams of western Elaptirius, having a high habit of finding children that had gone astray, and tempting them into his service. These stray Passians were not mutilated and tortured like the Desiroth, so we must conclude that the terms agreed upon by Caldar and Alyin forbade it. Caldar came to call this second group of followers the Stremianair, for they were fair and more agile of body.

The Fourth Age began around the year 900, and while it refers chiefly to the Nephinarthins in the East and their organization as a sophisticated culture, so too in the West did society begin to build upon itself at this time. The greatest gem of civilization here came to be a kingdom called ALYINEN, which was headed by none other than Alyin the Starling, who took a member of the Riverguard, Mandle of Arthle, to be her prince. They founded their kingdom far away from the memory of Caldar's Crossing upon the Urf, tucked deep in a southern corner of the continent, between the Sestarions and the great Southern Woods. Here, it is said the first tall structure of any kind was built upon earth, a mighty castle for the Goddess Alyin and her King Mandle. Though the entire kingdom was fated to be razed and washed out completely by the winds of time, some will still say that the deepest foundations of modern-day Shynin Or belong to that magical kingdom of Alyinen.

The year was 939. Caldar, then resting peacefully enough in the Tredellian Valleys, was infuriated when he at last caught the news of Alyin's binding herself to a Passian and making her own kingdom upon earth, which he considered to be a breach of her promises, whatever they might have been. Swiftly Caldar sent down emissaries, his Stremianair servants, to declare war upon the Kingdom of Alyinen should his ancient affection not denounce her claim.

She did not. And so Caldar marched forth again, with a doubled army and the support of fresh recruits ranging from the north valleys to the land of Rolling Reed who had nothing better to fight for. They arrived at the gates of Alyinen, finding a glimmering land beyond, with a castle not yet complete lying in a bare plain surrounded by rolling yellow hills. Caldar growled and held tight the reigns of his dear steed Lontik, and bellowed out a full force attack upon all that stood within the kingdom's gates.

King Mandle fought bravely enough, but the land was not on his side. For the Kingdom of Alyinen, though pristine and beautiful to behold, rest atop an endless bog, which lie just steps beneath the thin layer of flower and grass. And so as the men began to fall, the armies of Caldar would smash them down into the sinking grounds, and the earth would devour them. This proved to be disheartening for Mandle and his soldiers, and morale quickly deteriorated— before they realized it, they were half of them drowning in marsh, their bodies to be frozen in pain and sadness until the day when many of them would be uncovered by curious folk in the much-later fortress of Shynin Or.

Mandle submitted himself on bended knee before Caldar just before moonrise, in the midst of a circle of wailing Desiroth. The negotiations were short, for little was Mandle's position for bargain. In order that Caldar might disband his army and leave Alyinen in peace— and vow never to return— then Mandle must willingly climb into his own coffin and lie still while his brothers bury him in hot black sand.

Mandle accepted on the condition that he might have one more night with Alyinen. Caldar refused.

But he did declare that pain would never come to the queen by his hand so long as she remained within her kingdom. And so, restraining his sorrow, Mandle rose slowly, taking in one last look at the bright orange sun resting wide atop the southern horizon.

In the long stone hall of his castle, patches of roof lying yet bare, Mandle waded between his six brothers, the six which survived the battle. A hissing Desiroth— with two small mouths and a rotten bare bone between them— smiled as best as one like that can, and opened a shining gold casket for the First King of Alyinen. Mandle climbed inside; his brother handed him his sword. Mandle closed his eyes, and clutched the sword, gently moving one hand down its steel silver blade. He glided his hand along it several times, as though savoring every speck of time that he had left to feel the familiar with his fingers, hoping perhaps that he could take any feeling at all with him to what lie beyond.

Three of his fingers at last lifted off the silver blade— the fourth lingering a moment more, and then, as soon as his palm rested still upon the hilt— black sand covered all his skin. Alyin stood by the door, looking in as her king was scorched and buried alive in the hall he had himself only begun to build. As Caldar approached, he muttered only a snide remark, to which Alyin turned, not looking at any part of him.

For those of my readers who are unable to detect pattern, let me say that firstly, if you cannot yet see a pattern between Caldar and Alyin, you are horrendously dim. But I hope by this point you can see that the actions Caldar were always influenced by his standing with Alyin, and whether justifiable or not, this is how it was. His attack on her kingdom had settled his rage for a moment, but nothing was truly resolved, and so soon he began to drive horror across the lands once more.

Glitharog was laid bare, with fire scorching the earth to its bone. Gwidenarsa was swallowed whole, with all its peoples carried away to delve mines in the Western Sashites. Indeed, these were dark times for all north of Alyinen's border. South of that border, however, Alyin remained in her realm, which prospered under a new line of kings.

On Risenwood

It is said the greatest heroes arise out of the black of the greatest darkness. Perhaps the notion first began with the ascension of Havoth of Hildor, a broad-shouldered wielder of a sword that stretched up twice his own height, who would head the daring resistance to the Lord of All Evil. Many in my day have rejected the idea that one man led the army of thousands — all those who praised Tiluma in the West— and that this image of valiant Havoth was brewed up from a natural desire to provide the innumerous heroes of the Caldarian Opposition with a face of their own, one that would echo down through millennia.

The Caldarian Opposition sent pleas to all the great chieftains in Gandrypool and Glitharog— the response was thin. They then looked to the growing city of Furin Weed, nearby and with great stocks of weapons and horses. But none in Furin Weed appeared at the assembled council; instead they all hid among the tall blades in their watery channels. Havoth of Hildor was furious, and roared that if ever the dreaded curse of Caldar be lifted from their lands, he would then spare no hurt in dealing with the cowards of Furin Weed.

But a miraculous thing happened which would more than compensate for the cowardice of the channel dwellers and all men afar. The men of Bludor— not just the wermen, but the women, and the children— stepped forward with an oath of allegiance. And with them they brought a wild host of distant relatives who had long dwelled north in the Green Woods.

Together they marched to Risenwood, a modest mound with a covering of great oaks and pines, not but a mile off the shores of the Glimmer. Here they clashed with Caldar, who held both the high ground and the Livyer Staff— an unstoppable combination. Victory was unobtainable. Through a night that lasted three days, with an unpenetrable black cloud blocking all light, the Caldarian Opposition sprinted rank after rank up the hills of Risenwood.

The charges were fruitless. No matter the number, Caldar would strike them down with ease; nor did it matter from which direction they came. Even when all forces diverged on Caldar at once, from all sides, he would merely swing round his staff and send their bones barreling from their bodies. He also commanded great flashes of fire, which he summoned from above in the form of lightning at first, but soon grew tired of the formalities and simply ignited bare flame for the remainder of the fight.

All the hill of Risenwood burned. Seen from the Glimmer, those armies that were reluctant to join now saw no just cause. To put forth their aid would be to literally walk into a raging firestorm— a challenge which only the men of Bludor were eager enough to accept. And accept it they did, not just with the same dense tactics as those already perishing on the hill, but with the ingenuity to scale the trees and attack Caldar from above. This is how the day was at last won, with the noble folk of Bludor quietly climbing the pines of Risenwood, many of them suffocating in the thick smoke from the continuously rising flame, and then all leaping down on Caldar at once from above his head, a place he did not expect.

With his Livyer Staff confiscated, Caldar bore little more power than what the strength of fourteen men could supply, and so the fight was not long after that. Havoth, who had commanded his ranks from the safety of a ship on the bank of the Glimmer, now rushed up onto the hill to deliver a final blow to Caldar, although mere blows are not sufficient in the killing of a Starling. So Havoth and the folk of Bludor resolved to bind him with chain and place him a coffin, entombing him deep in the earth and tending the land so that none would reach him, nor he would ever escape. This was to serve as an eternal punishment, for his heinous treachery, fashioned after the storied damnation of Gelseth, which all of them knew well.

And thus Caldar was imprisoned. We are not certain the year, for the calendars of this ancient region are lost to us, if they had any at all. Though we can surmise that this First Fall of Caldar occurred probably somewhere between the years 1000 and 1100. This would be in line with the time in which the territories of Gandrypool and Glitharog began to surge in coordination, with evidence of mass famine, sickness, and genocide also coinciding in this period.

We are also told that Caldar had, for at least a couple of hundred years, served his sentence when the fateful year of 1333 would arrive.

On Darifath

Darifath was born in the Corn Havens, around the year 1300. Unloved by his peers, he became a creature of sorrow and misery. History knows not the name of Darifath's affection, for his standing never rose to great heights, and his words would've been ill-respected by any chronicler of his day. We do now, however, from later words of Caldar, know that Darifath would sit long hours in the corn and even by night, waiting for the unpredictable moment when his affection would pass by, hoping that one day she might speak to him, though she never did.

Darifath heard the legends of Caldar from an early age, and how he was not so very evil at all in the start. He always believed that Caldar in fact had once been a very good being, deterred only by loneliness and sorrow, as he himself felt.

And so he set out. To find Caldar, and set him loose.

He walked east, coming to what we now know as the Bear Stretch, but in those long forgotten days, that country was the pumping heart of Gandrypool. What happened to turn the tide on such ancient settlements as Havothroc, Tilumasun, and Brundun we will soon come to.

But as Darifath walked across these peaceful towns, set amongst green pastures lying between low bouldered valleys, he was stopped by many who meant to do him harm. For he should not, by any means said they, walk alongside the Urf toward the Glimmer and on to the Tomb of Caldar in Risenwood. He was told that multiple children had walked to the place of Caldar's imprisonment over the course of years, lured by sinister promises through the wind. They were all of them afflicted with various ailments of the flesh, and died not long thereafter, only by standing near to the ground where the dark lord lie.

Darifath told those he encountered that they had nothing to fear— he hadn't really any desire to set eyes upon the Tomb of Caldar, yet alone free him. Not after the horrible tales he had heard now of his deeds before the days of his imprisonment: of his rounding up sons from their mothers, never to return, or of his creatings of foul beasts that would stain the land and torture the living, forcing many from their homes. Yet despite these assurances, Darifath would not turn homeward. He had come far, and nothing at all would've been accomplished in his mind to return to his dreadful existence in the Corn Havens. He longed to look upon the face of Caldar in secret, and to hear his forked words against his own ears. Perhaps he thought he could truly revert him back to some semblance of light.

After trekking up the Urf, Darifath arrived on the Glimmer Lake near the High of Wethember, when the days would have been longest and warmest. He dined upon the shores of the popular water, a rival to the Nephin Bay, though a world away. Here, one might assume that the endless accounts of curious and stupid children scaling the grounds of Risenwood to catch glimpse of Caldar's Tomb would be enough to deter Darifath's goal, for again he was told that none of the children came back the same, albeit this time by grieved mothers and kin. Most never came back at all, they weeped, but all who did were either missing in limbs or in spirits.

There were no roads to Risenwood from any of the cities along the Glimmer— all had been destroyed intentionally to make any attempt at reaching Caldar all but impossible. The foolish children had all swam across the lake to find him, but this would prove difficult for Darifath, who knew not how to swim. Oh how the fate of the world might have been completely changed, if upon that night he set out, a fisher had not left his boat unchained to his dock, enabling a swift and stealthy Darifath to steal away into the night.

He rowed the boat to the middle of the lake, where the bottom rises to a notoriously shallow sand, and then carried the boat overhead until the bed gave out beneath him and he was almost drowned in the deep of the drop-off. But he clutched the side of the boat and through his determination of bettering life he pulled himself up, riding the belly of the capsized vessel towards Risenwood, which lay in a cove past many twists in the lake. Had his luck been any worse, day would have come and the patrols on the waters would have carried him away for his attempt. But Darifath made it to Risenwood with an hour of black to spare.

Stepping onto the ledge of land, there were many warning signs to be spotted, all written in blood. Darifath had no time for reading, lest his quest be in vain. And so he trudged up the overgrown hill, which used to hold a narrow path— all was planted over with dense and tangling vines to deter would-be trespassers. But the vines had never stopped the foolish children, nor would they stop Darifath, who slashed his way through until he did come to a steep path, with long wooden steps placed apart at great distance, leading up towards moon and stars, seen above the pines shooting out from the hillside.

The final obstacle when Darifath at last reached the peak of Risenwood was the clever tomb that Havoth and his men had constructed to contain Calder— an encirclement of thick trees, planted so close together that by this time they had run up into one another, leaving only narrow spaces of an inch or so between. None had yet succeeded in passing this tree hurdle into the ground within where Caldar lie; ground which Darifath could see by putting one eye up to a crack.

From that blackened ground within, a voice groaned. But as Darifath made his introduction, the voice turned to song. A mournful sigh and a tune of ancient sadness swept through the pines, and as light began to thrust momentum over morning clouds, a wave of color struck the face of Darifath. He bowed low on the ground, submitting his thoughts to the words of Caldar.

"You are in anguish," spoke Caldar from beneath the ground. "This is why you travel far. It is not for love of the road, but for love of what might be, if only you had the means to submit them to your will."

"I would release you, Caldar," spoke Darifath, "If not for the tales of children who wandered up this hill in years past; why have you struck them with such sickness?"

Softly, Caldar replied, "They were not come with pure intention to release me, as you so valiantly have. Rather, they came only with wicked hearts, led by dare or test of bravery to exhilarate their thirst for danger and rebellion against the wishes of their mothers. They came to snicker between the cracks where your eyes now rest, gazing upon a being condemned to lie in ground, never dying, with nothing but doomed thought to crowd his company. They hid their fear behind veils of laughter, tempting one another to see who might get closest to the humming groan of the ground. And so I smote them all with burning cyst."

"That's fair," nodded Darifath. "Children are cruel. I always thought so, though I never was. It seems we may have much in common, Caldar. If I were to uncover your coffin, and crack it open, what would then become of me?"

"What would you wish, Darifath of Corn Haven?"

"The lady of my affection, who has not once stopped upon seeing me alone on the Cornstalk Path. Surely you know of how I feel, for I have heard many times the tale of yourself and Alyin. They are quite popular among the Havens, and all heard them from childhood."

Caldar was stung deep at the mention of Alyin, and his mood towards Darifath shifted then, though he did not show it. Instead, he remained composed and instructed Darifath to embark now for the stronghold at Havothroc, where Caldar's great staff was taken after his defeat. When Darifath inquired at how he knew this, Caldar spoke that the words of Kezhil still haunted his dreams, for the spirit of Kezhil sees all, and through him his powers are renewed. So would Darifath be granted such powers if he succeeded in this task of retrieving the staff.

And so Darifath sped away, back down the road whence he came, and arrived at Havothroc to inquire of the legendary Staff of Caldar.

"You cannot have it," he was told.

Well, then Darifath would be in need craftiness. He cleverly devised to light the whole town ablaze, and amidst the havoc of burning Havothroc, he swam upstream directly into its main hall. There he put out the eyes of the town's master with two sticks, and took the Livyer Staff for himself.

Darifath attempted to shove the great staff down his pocket so as to avoid detection as he hiked back up the Urf, but the Livyer Staff is ten feet tall, and therefore did not fit in his pocket. Instead, he broke into a butcher's shop and hid the staff within a great bear carcass. Now it was only a matter of getting a great bear carcass to Risenwood.

He used a cart. And with sweat streaming down his face in the relentless heat of Wethember, he pushed along the bear, going by the mercy of moonlight most often, and took the long way around the Glimmer— the dense, roadless wooded way— to avoid the water and also the men.

Now then, after this slight divergence, Darifath climbed the steps of Risenwood a second time, this time with the powerful staff in his hands, which did nothing for him, for he knew not how it worked. He stopped again at the crack in the trees before Caldar's resting spot, but he had grown more bitter since his first visit. Perhaps it was pushing a great bear's carcass uphill for many miles and then stomping across fly-infested backwoods to get to a place he had already been. But no matter the reason, this time he had more on his mind and would speak it clearly.

"I will release you, Lord Caldar, to be sure. But I have my conditions. I will only release you," said Darifath with gravitas, "If you promise to win for me the lady of my affection, but also to make her pay for her past indifference. And to especially make ruin of those who courted her before."

He hesitated, and Caldar assumed that he was done. But still Darifath continued. "And to all those who scorned me in my hour of misery, I wish for them to be banished. For the Corn Havens I will have as my own. And I'd have you come every season to remind my subjects of your terrible fury. Demonstrate for them your majestic powers, and that if my will not be done, they'll be on the wrong end of it. And if I could have a share of your secrets, perhaps something of a Livyer Staff of my own, I would appreciate— well, I demand that too, for if you don't swear it then I simply won't release you."

He went on like this for hours. And at last Caldar could hear no more. He promised that all would be done. And so Darifath cast the Livyer Staff between the crack in the trees, and it landed upon the dark bitter land between. The ground began to bubble, wetting itself and dissolving, until a leathery reptilian hand began to emerge slowly through the soil. The claws gripped the staff, and all the mud began to part. Caldar rose, shining in black glory, with white strands of ghostly grandeur flailing out in the wind, just as they had done on the night of his Crossing nearly 600 years ago. The thick trees parted enough for Darifath to enter and fall to his knees, his eyes blinded by the light of his dark lord.

As Darifath opened his mouth to speak again, Caldar silenced him and bade a great horn to sprout from his back— as a showing of his great power and dominance, as well as his anger for Darifath's pride and arrogance. He did not stop there, for the eyes of Darifath then ruptured, spilling out acidic rains from the sockets. His hands then crumpled and he fell forward, to move about as a beast on hooves. Many other mutilations occurred that night, until Darifath became what we now commonly know to be the Dath; that is, the hideous demon that Caldar employs in his service to go about his business, sending him upon houses who speak ill of his name, to drag them out into the night and clamp on their necks with its clattering clipper of a beak.

So Darifath's tale, then, does not end well. It is still being told, though, for one thing that Caldar did grant to him was the power of an unwithering body, which might be seen as more of a curse than a gift.

I have devoted a full chapter to this tale because the daring quest of this doomed soul enabled all the rest of history to transpire as it has, for the influence of Caldar would now spread into the East. And there it would collide with another force, one who would prove to be his equal in battle, indeed the only living creature on the face of the earth to meet his match in power, of body or of mind.

On Melizar

Here we must again take back to more ancient hours. In the waning days of the First Age.

If Caldar was the origin of all evil on earth, than Melizar is its perfection, taking it from strides of narrow-minded anger and wrath into complex fields of scheming, manipulation, and complete flaying of the spirit.

She was a soft and gentle Primordial Starling of the Eastern Green Woods, that most pleasant haven of crisp palms blowing in breeze and emitting precious mist and aroma, and blameless was she from the beginning of all malice and guilt.

But near the ending of the First Age, when across the world Caldar had begun to mingle his thoughts with Kezhil, she was changed, or perhaps merely awoken. For the spirits of evil and hatred and desire curled forward out of Caldar's mind like twisted wave, and blew on the winds eastward, towards Melizar's corner of the woods. Other Starlings there acknowledged the peculiar scent of the winds blowing through, but none said the more. Melizar, on other breast, inhaled the winds to no end.

She liked how it felt. The calm breezes that brushed against her skin were no longer enough to please her fully. If these winds would try so hard, finding their way between the palms to reach her, then could she not bring her fellow lifelings to do the same? The winds could be manipulated to an entirely different purpose, she now thought, for she now saw that she was beautiful, and that all existence ought to have been created to please her. The level grass and forest floor now seemed to slant a slope, and there was serenity only atop, where she resolved to be.

Her fellow Starlings were now grown ugly in the mind of Melizar, who began to declare her own face to be that of the perfection that Tiluma had meant to carry out in the beginning, but had failed to duplicate. And the Starlings believed her. As they came to accept Melizar's exceptional beauty, so the Starlings saw themselves more and more imperfect in the mirrored streams of the Green Woods, and their thoughts linked with their flesh. They lost much of their glow, and their faces sank into hollow remnants of what they once were; this is why the few Starlings that survive today appear not much more than pretty Passians.

For many years then Melizar reigned as a goddess among all in that corner of the woods. Her beauty was unopposed, her words unchallenged. And she had the Starlings and dark-skinned Passians that dwelt there serve her at all hours of the day, having them labor in the sun and touch her in gentle praise within a moment of her command.

But still Melizar's thirst would not be quenched. Nor would it ever be, for that is the nature of her spirit. Even if all the world, along with all the stars and all the gods, were to fall flat before her in absolute surrender, with sun and moon falling into her teeth for her to taste in entirety, still would she look on for a new conquest.

And so, the total devotion of her people not sufficient in pleasing her, Melizar would steal away, abandoning her bed in the clearing, where slaves of her will would wait patiently for her return, and she would find a cave. For there, trapped inside, were the winds of evil, desire, lust, malice— all things were new and released into the air when Caldar's thoughts mingled with Kezhil. And Melizar gasped in ecstasy, clenching her teeth, biting down hard on her tongue, letting out a laugh as these vibrant winds shook her. And with them she would roll in gentle thrust every moment eyes did not watch, letting the time pass slow, letting the darkness tickle her in deep places, in caverns and in pits. On stone tables she would spin, every moment growing louder, her voice turning into that of a feral beast, barking and roaring through the cave, clawing at bone— an orgasm of evil.

For many days and nights she slipped away to her caves and did exactly as I have described, unnoticed. But being so beloved by her peoples, it was inevitable that one day her followers would follow her to her place of sinful escape. This group of men stood silent, confused, and violated outside the mouth of the cave, as they heard their empress screaming out horrendous cries, cursing all the earth and damning every living soul, imploring that they all die for her and then be reborn by her command, to be tied and bound by string, held in her fingers for all time.

As Melizar emerged from the cave naked, the group of curious Passians looked on her for explanation. She was out of breath, and at a lack for words. She fled in the woods, and this group of folk— the Witnesses— tried to make sense of what they had seen. They told their fellow men back in the woods, for their adoration of Melizar had been broken after hearing her vile words from outside the cave.

Though the Starlings and Passians were not swayed away from their loyalty— they had not witnessed anything, after all— Melizar was still wary of this spreading testimony. She knew she needed to silence this group of Witnesses, to stop the spread of any ill word against her that might spread. And so in a public bathing ceremony— which were commonplace, for all who gaze upon Melizar desire nothing else than to partake in bathing her— Melizar talked long about the colors of the world, and how green was fine, but there was far too much of it. It had become dull, for it was all they ever saw, beside the grey of the sky and the brown of the dirt.

She. then told her followers of the color red. At first they did not understand. Which is fair; one cannot so easily understand a color by description if they have nothing with which to reference the color. And truly, nothing in their midst was red. So the Witnesses were called forward.

"Since you, my loyal and eternal slaves, are failing to comprehend what I describe, I will show you. Come forth, Passian."

And she dug her fingers into the wrist of one of the Witnesses — Dimad was his name— and Dimad bled. All around looked on, surprised. "This is red," declared Melizar, her golden body resting in white basin, "And it is my most favorite of colors."

Immediately upon her saying so, the forest followers of Melizar began to find the blood in their own bodies, and lay it before her willingly. Melizar laughed. "The one who can show me the most red will gain an eternal place at my side, to be the sole giver of my baths."

And the ripping of flesh grew more rapid and fierce. Soon all Passians present were dead. The Starlings, however, do not have an ounce of red in their bodies, so they did not rip into their skin. It would have been pointless. And so they survived, for the time being.

Yet the falling of the Passians unsettled the Eastern Starlings. They were not sure why, yet, for they did not comprehend death— but the Passians would no longer respond to touch, and their bodies began to rot, which was enough to make the Starlings know that it was not a good thing that was done.

Immediate action was not taken against Melizar for the same reason that action was not taken against Tiluma after he damned away Gelseth. It is a fearful thing to rise against great power when great cruelty is known to be the price.

For years, the power of Melizar in that part of the world was total and complete. But, as earlier stated, it is not in the character of Melizar to ever be contented, and so an upward climb was initiated in her heart, in a never-ceasing effort to keep all her deepest desires satiated. The demands that she pressed upon the Passians in her midst were appalling— yet they complied, for the very thought of disobeying the one who claimed dominion over them seemed to be the most heinous deed imaginable.

The adoration and compliance of her many hundreds of worshippers was not enough, however. She aimed to turn the number to thousands. While at the same time performing four daily sacrifices— one at the point when the sky was brightest, one for when the sky was most dark, and two others at the points in between. Melizar endeavored always to keep the sacrifices fresh and inventive, but her favorite has come down to us as a vivid memory in the hearts of the Hayamese, who would soon flee her presence.

She would demand the sacrificial Passian to stand with head tilted full back, so that the mouth— the airway of the praises that were due to the self-proclaimed goddess— pointed directly up at the sky. A second man was then made to take a tall and smooth hollowed-out branch, and to force it down into the throat of the sacrifice. The branch would be maneuvered down the airway to the very source of the voice, and there would connect with the soul. Now the second Passian would bend the branch, bending the sacrifice's head backward, until the airway now faced directly into the ground. In this way the voice and the praises to Melizar would therefore be diverted from the sky, back into the ground, where lies the sacred Kingdom of Margon, awaiting its day of rebirth. Often times the head of the sacrificial Passian would snap clear off the neck; this is bound to happen to all but the most flexible and freak-worthy of bodies when pushed far enough.

After years of witnessing this obscene ritual— years of witnessing the heads of their kin snapped off in an ill twist, years of veins tearing and spilling blood upon Melizar's thirsty hands— a small faction of the Passians there realized that this was no sensical course of existence.

Wilgo Bothgo is the werman credited with starting the first migration of peoples out of Melizar's grasp, and thus commencing the SECOND AGE of this world. For Bothgo brought forth several splendid ideas to his fellow Passians, namely that to live in perpetual submission to Melizar would bring them inevitably to a grizzly execution, and to live there in rebellion of Melizar would bring them to an even swifter execution. So the only real option they had in the interest of their own preservation was to flee.

Still, many of those whom Wilgo Bothgo counseled found no need for self-preservation. They saw their passing lives as only a means to please the glory of Melizar, and only found happiness in the idea that their meager forms might play a role, however small, in her supreme existence. And so the night before Bothgo led his brethren out of Melizar's woods, these subservients hobbled to their goddess on bended knee— offering a sacrifice of 128 for good measure— and brought to her the tidings of the betrayal that Wilgo Bothgo meant to enact.

The following day, Melizar feigned sleep, allowing Bothgo to depart the woods with his followers, numbered at about six hundred. I made that number up. I have no idea really, no one does. It is recorded nowhere. Any source that claims to know the number of those in Wilgo Bothgo's company is outright lying to you. But surely it must've been a fine migration for the story to have come down to us from an age of which we have so little detail.

Anycourse, the tales do record that Bothgo led his folk down to the Ford of Hestleren. He, like those he led, must've been utterly clueless as to where to go, being as he was part of the first handful of generations to ever live. And indeed these primordial Passians had never wandered far from Melizar's woods— this was their first great migration. And sadly short-lived it would prove to be.

For Melizar chased them to the Falls of Thacban, which have ever since been named the Falls of Thacban for the fact that Melizar's followers purportedly flew in on the backs of Thacban— they being the great winged serpents belonging to the more legendary days of this world. Now, to clear up some common misconceptions on the Thacban beast, they were indeed capable of breathing flame. Though this has become misconstrued by many, who conclude that breathing and shooting out are one and the same. They are not. So while the winged Thacban serpents could inhale fire quite effortlessly, it would be utterly ridiculous to assume that they could spit fire outward from their mouths. However, they could regurgitate Kundra on a whim, and this in many ways was worse.

For Kundra is a sticky substance, which will work its way in between the pores of a man's skin, and will bring forth havoc to a Passian's body. Within hours, the bones of one afflicted will dissolve entirely— but only the bones— leaving the skin and organs fully intact, to lie on the ground in a shapeless and writhing form.

This is what became of the Passian migrants led under Wilgo Bothgo, who found themselves covered in Thacban vomit, and then an hour later found themselves to be still with all the energies of life, but simply without structure. For they were then boneless men, and able to be easily picked away by the smallest of birds with beaks. This was what Melizar desired, and if she had had her way to the fullest, the migration plotted by Bothgo would have ended their. But the regurgitation of the Thacban Kundra was at last too much for many of her followers to stomach.

The lifelings in the Eastern Green Woods were split in two. Half now saw the cruelty of Melizar's ways, while half still clung to their love of her dominance, for nothing would sway them now. A great battle erupted on one starlit night, and many were slain by sword and Thacban, but those who escaped fled with speed, and did not stop running until they reached the Andiloth. Indeed, those who escaped the grasp of Melizar had to be fast, and it is because of this that their descendants are still today marked among the swiftest of men. These descendants eventually settled amidst the Great Sands south of the Kyseth Dead Lands, and spread westward to the fertile lands south of the Belltop Mountains. They came to found the nation of Hayaman, and in this way all the truest of the Hayamese hold the tradition that they once stood defiantly against Melizar and departed forever from her presence.

Those who stayed within that presence would be the fathers of Ancient Pendala, and their descendants would continue to worship the image of their perfect Starling.

Two thousands or so after the departure of the Hayamese from Pendala, Melizar came to make her own departure. She had grown at last tired of the green of the red— the green of the trees and the red of the sacrificial blood— and so she walked ever southward, finding all the lands there to be dull and of little interest, until she came to the jagged rocks of Ansila. These will be described in greater detail in the chapters concerning the War of Haegos, for it is here that Melizar set up her permanent dwelling. And here, that in the year 1431, she gazed across the sky in wonder as a fierce display of lightworks transpired, culminating in a vast black cyclone. All in that part of Denderrin Othim were witness to this strange spectacle, the likes of which were never seen again until my Eleventh Age. We know the year was 1431 for the Nephinarthins courteously took the time to take their own note of it.

It was Caldar and his Desiroth legions, newly reclaimed and wandering eastward across the earth, that set about the famous lightworks. Never one to boast the powers granted to him by his powerful staff, Caldar nonetheless set the lightworks in motion to declare to Denderrin Othim his coming, so that any who sought an audience with this great sorcerer might now present themselves. Melizar did exactly that, wandering with her host of Pendalese out of Ansila Siroth, and meeting her unknown counterpart on the slopes of Stellis, the great volcanic peak at the end of the Red Canyons.

"You must be a great sorceror indeed to summon such spectacle into an otherwise dull sky," spoke Melizar upon meeting Caldar for the first.

"I am the lord of all evil upon this world," spoke Caldar plainly, not wishing to boast but rather to simply relay a fact.

But Melizar smirked, not to be outdone. "It was I who first diverted from the plans of Tiluma. I stand alone among our race, for I first mingled with dark winds, and without my malice, all in this corner of the world would still be in balance."

Here, their stately meeting dissolved into unending squabble, with both Caldar and Melizar claiming to be the source of all evil, and then Melizar claiming to be the most evil, a title which Caldar heeded to her willingly, for he believed this to be true. But still he claimed to be the source, which Melizar would not have. In the heat of the argument, she then stepped forth quite unexpectedly, to grab Caldar by force and plant his lips upon her own, to which Caldar quickly dodged and sent Melizar tripping down the slopes.

Melizar was appalled, for not in over a hundred years had one denied her lips. And now she craved the dark lord in her midst even more, though she did not show it. For Caldar was resilient to her ways, and for all his reputation as the source of all evil, he strangely did not show it. In some ways, he may have grown virtuous since his imprisonment upon Risenwood. Whatever the state of Caldar's mind, he simply found nothing desirable in the being called Melizar, and this drove the Queen of Darkness into a frenzy.

For the better part of a hundred years, Melizar interrogated her sister Starlings of the West, learning all there was to know on the tale of Caldar and Alyin. Jealousy raged in the bowels of Melizar, for she realized that Caldar's passion was yet too great and devoted to this Alyin for him to ever break its bonds. At last Melizar offered to bind Alyin outright and deliver her to Caldar, on the condition that Caldar engage in Melizar's desires for the span of a single season. Even this Caldar refused, and so Melizar waged war upon her primordial kin.

Thirty-one years was the allotted time to gather their forces, and those forces would be enough to baffle all the subsequent ages of man.

On The Grand Battle of Athuka

Never was a larger force ever assembled and brought to war across the many faces of the earth as here. No single battle ever lent more numbers into fight; the only thing comparable would be The Battle of Angelon which took place in my own time, but that is assuming the figures of Athuka are stretched (which they very well could be; ancient chroniclers are not known for their accuracy and honest reporting). However, if we are to believe the first-hand accounts, even for a moment, then this battle pitted nine million against an even larger fifteen million. Caldar held the nine, Melizar the fifteen. And Caldar might have won, outnumbered as he was, if the battle was fought through strictly fair means, though we could never hold Melizar to that end, for devious means are her craft.

Now, one may well bring the scale of the battle into immediate question by pointing out that twenty-million soldiers is an even greater number of total people living in all of Elaptirius today. A very true fact, but that is not taking into account all the ancient beasts that roamed the world in those days. Ancient Thacban, Ekwin, Chipperin, Gar Loly, Cooskan Parse, Desiroth, Stremianair, Brundlecock, sentient Horglefunt, Bear

People, Wolf-Men, Foxian, Starling, Passian, Buffits, Wengs—all were present for this great engagement.

Such was why they chose the Plains of Athuka for their conflict — a seemingly endless stretch of barren flat land would provide them with the perfect ground for fair fight, which this battle was devised to be. And as the endless sea of soldiers amassed, their cries of war were deafening. They yelled out curse upon curse at their opponents, and all forgot the very existence of silence. This went on for about three hours, or three months— the word in the lone ancient manuscript is smudged and it could be either or, we can't entirely tell. But at last came the great moment for the two leaders to step forward.

Caldar made his entrance simply enough, with his great hoards parting for him as he descended out of a great wooden wolf. He marched into the empty void simply enough, for this battle was not of his devising. He was simply caught up in the midst of Melizar's hatred and jealousy, and his own following that would not stand for Melizar's lordship.

Melizar made a more lavish entrance, as she arrived upon an enormous statue of a Thacban, made of pure ice. Atop the ice was a platform reaching far into the sky, and as she approached Athuka, Melizar stepped out of her tent— her great antlered helmet resting atop her proud head, which betrayed no emotion— and gazed down upon Caldar, standing alone between the two raging forces, ready for battle.

Upon descending her magnificent Thacban of Ice, Caldar spared no moments for ceremony. He immediately engaged Melizar with a swing of the sword, and battle was commenced. Melizar is said to have caught the blow with her hands, and as the blade ripped upon between her fingers and nails, she decried Caldar as an abomination of creation. Here, the two sides converged without mercy, and the souls of 21 million were cast into an earthly ring of hell.

We can only guess as to how the tides of that truly massive battle flowed, but it was eventually the forces of Melizar that triumphed, for she summoned the Windfolk, or in other words cheated Caldar out of victory. For the Windfolk are not folk at all, but rather simply gusts of wind, which when brought under command can prove fatal to any army. Melizar claimed ever after that her summoning of the Windfolk was in no way foul play, for she held that they were merely apparitions of spirits once living, and therefore had every right to participate in the great battle.

And so Caldar was defeated on the Plains of Athuka, his armies decimated except for the back ranks of Desiroth and Stremianair, which fled well before the Summoning of the Windfolk. Caldar was then brought chained to Melizar, who violated him for a time in her tall tower at Ansila Siroth. But still did she desire to him suffer more than anything else, for his prior rejections of her advances, and so she made ready a second coffin for Caldar's imprisonment.

To heighten the sting to unbearable lengths— for it was not enough to Melizar that Caldar once again be imprisoned under the earth— she brought forth Alyin, who had been wandering the dark, cloudy shores of Dunothim for some past centuries. Now at last Caldar gazed upon his great love, whom he had not seen in many an age. And Alyin looked back at Caldar, truly this time, and perhaps at last seeing that his original intents were not as vile as she had assumed in that primordial forest, so many thousands of years back. At any rate, Caldar's villainy now paled in comparison with that Melizar.

These may have been the thoughts of Alyin as she briefly found herself within Ansila Siroth; who are we to say. But within moments of being brought before Caldar, Alyin's throat was then slit, and her throat torn out by Melizar's Pendalese servants. Her heart was then bashed in with an obsidian stone, and her face feasted on by an especially hungry crow, who just happened to appear in the window. All this happened within moments, and then Caldar was cast into a coffin, and the corpse of Alyin thrown in on top of him.

In this way, Caldar was made to endure his second imprisonment in the year 1556, shortly after losing the Grand Battle of Athuka. His coffin was carried out of Ansila Siroth, and buried in an unknown spot, deep within the dense and mangled trees of the Shilong Forest.

But, luckily for Caldar— who still wasn't all that lucky, what with being locked away in a coffin under the corpse of his one love— he was not to wait much longer than a single century this time before he was once again set loose. The precise year is in doubt, but once again children made their way to the resting place of the dark lord, for they were led on by the whispers and dares all the same. It was a young boy and girl— Sieclin and Seclina— who wandered into Shilong one day and followed the moaning earth to Caldar's ground. They spent an entire night uncovering him, for they were only children and not skilled in digging deep holes. But when the task was finally done, and the dark lord rose just as he did with Darifath, Sieclin and Seclina thrusted their pits with joy.

And Caldar repaid these children well. He did nothing to them of heinous nature, for he was grown tired of devastation. The past century spent lying in a grave with Alyin's corpse had rid his desire for her, and he had worked out several dilemmas within his own mind in the time of his second imprisonment. Now Caldar and the children of his liberation walked through the woods as friends, Caldar doing much to ward off the beasts of the forest that had so haunted Sieclin and Seclina in the days beforehand.

Upon returning to civilized lands, Caldar learned that the previous century had been primarily concerned with the murdering of his Starling brethren, all at the hands of Athuka's victor. Those few Starlings who managed to survive the Purging of Melizar escaped to lands far and wide, eventually settling predominantly in the Miller's Wood, just south of the gates to Hildor. There they reside to this day; I have seen them myself. They are real.

But seeing as though Melizar had so effectively rid the world of almost all her kind, Caldar— not wanting to be caught up in the genocide— remained quiet and traveled all the world extensively, content to see the new wonders that had sprung up in the waning days of the Fourth Age. He would not come to see the Rise of Therok and Angelon, however, for in 1756— a mere eight years before Thellig would claim his rock— Caldar was once again hunted.

This time it was Brillac, long haired but not of the head, who would chase Caldar across field and stream, to the farthest reaches of the untamed West.

"All the discord that you have witnessed here," yelled Brillac the Boundless as he cornered Caldar upon Rocksend, "Is of your doing. If it were not for your vile existence, then all would be in peace! This world would have never known neither harsh winter nor burning summer, and all mothers would hold their children in peace, without fear of pain or death. The graves of all I lie upon your heart! You are the reason for sorrow, and all the cause of our suffering! And so I hunt you to this end, and charge you with a million woes, to be paid until the death of us all, and Margon rises from its pit!"

And with this impassioned speech, Brillac slayed Caldar at Rocksend, sending him into a third imprisonment, which would prove to be his longest. The coffin was this time carried to the Glimmer, though instead of being buried in Risenwood this time, the steel box was cast under the lake itself.

And there Caldar was thrown, to be held in that coffin for all time, never again to escape. And this has for the most part remained true and without incident, except for the recent culmination of the Eleventh Age, which has broken open many paths which never were thought to have been trodden down. I will leave the specifics to my later writing, where I detail my life's journeys in full, but I will foreshadow that there is a stunning tale of the idea of redemption, and the true meaning of genuine evil.

On the topic of genuine evil, without any bias in the equation, I should say that it is most finely represented in Melizar. For without ever having experienced a hardship (other than the tides of her wars) nor having been exposed to any form of loss, she continues to pursue endless praise to the devastation of all. And it is because of Melizar that we have leapt back to tell these tales of old, for she will come to factor in with the the heinous War of Haegos— the pinnacle of this manuscript— which I will begin at last to relate, now.

Part Four

The War of Haegos

Now at last we come to it. The darkest chapter in our history— not just that of the Kingdom of Angelon, but all the land of Elaptirius. For we hold in our hearts a collective understanding of that singular war, heinous above all others, and none of the fair could ever hear the name Haegos without rendering a shudder.

On Thaegoce

Where Caldar may be forgiven for his tragic tale, and Melizar for her blinding beauty, Haegos is in all ways reprehensible. Even from the eyes of a great redeemer, or from one of boundless empathy, the ways of Haegos are utterly unforgivable. Let us begin his tale when he was still called by his first name, which was Thaegoce, before he was forever changed by Melizar.

Thaegoce was the Fourth Duke of Mangiloth. And where other men might be described as layered, with nuances of dark and light defining an indescribable complexity of character, Thaegoce was by all accounts completely terrible. Born in 2202, Thaegoce showed little prospect from birth of being anything more than a lightly-buttered fecal tube upon crispened black bread.

For the feelings of others, he showed little regard. For the reasonings of others, he showed absolutely no regard, finding his own reason to be vastly superior in all things. His teachers of writing would exemplify great patience towards him— being richly satisfied in their occupations— but unlike many of the other Mangilothian children, Thaegoce refused to learn as things were taught. As for the letters of the Ferokian alphabet, he believed firmly that he would create his own symbols and, being as he was to be duke, all of Mangiloth would then calibrate to his reworkings. Upon constant assurances from his teachers that Mangiloth would not conform to a new alphabet simply because the duke willed it, Thaegoce would pout and cry, shortly thereafter erupting into screams and yells, running out into woods and rolling himself in mud so that his teachers would face the ripe wrath of his mother Seclina.

Seclina was an upright man of high order and cleanliness, and so to see her son— whom she ensured to be seen by all Mangiloth as a shining example of spotless grace— as a dirtied child wearing the earth, she would wrathen up wholly. The teachers would lose the positions and often their husbands, who were granted the choice of staying with their wives or becoming full residents at the Valcoss line of brothels. The loyal and wholesome of the husbands are said to have stayed with their decommissioned wives, only that a quick glance at the records of the times show that none of them proved to be as such.

When the new line of teachers at last grew short on the antics of Thaegoce, they would run forth and catch him before he could escape their walls, and Thaegoce would twist and bark ferociously, with the teachers holding onto his arm to prevent his escape. Thaegoce would then go to his mother Seclina and spread falsehoods of his teachers and peers openly assaulting him, grabbing his dukely arm by force and yanking on it— almost cracking it— and then whacking him like they would stomp the ass of a cat. Whether or not Seclina believed the words of her vile child, it's only guessing for us to say, but nonetheless she was ready to carry out punishment on those her son deemed it worthy of. And so all who had ever been charged with the touching of the future duke were taken to the Musical Prison, where heinous torture of the ear and mind was prevalent. Here, the same songs were played upon the same furdle, tobo, sloot, and parno— for all days until the instruments began to rot (at which point, there were more slithering insects on the instruments than wood).

All this time, Thaegoce's father Rancoth, the Third Duke of Mangiloth, was busied by his patrols on the border, where encroaching lands meant to diminish the power of the duchy. Forthright of these was Mangiloth's sister nation of Lycema, whose King Sashara held Rancoth in contempt for his treatment of the women in his court. For years, Rancoth had subdued not just a percentage, but all of the women in Mangiloth he could put his thumb upon to a life of sexual deeds, contrived solely for the pleasure of wermen. This, King Sashara found abhorrent enough, but it was at least confined to Rancoth's own people. But then Rancoth began to plunder the reaches of his neighbors, taking away their women too, and many ill-fated girls in the shallows of Lycema were abducted and brought deep into Mangiloth, and were never found again. This, King Sashara could not tolerate.

And so Lycema was now at war with Mangiloth, for the first handful of years in the 2200s. The great Kingdom of Angelon opted to stay fully out of these affairs, for then-king Wilderfrant V had already become popular by commanding the guarantee of his vendors that all their food and drink would be good, and thus did not want to risk his popularity by entering into a foreign conflict.

The brunt of the attacks on Mangiloth came from Enthin Croth, a great long and black fortress that stood behind a marsh, in wide sight of the Mangiloth border. Behind Enthin Croth lay the great cavernous country of white hills collectively known as the Hollow Rounds. And so while Thaegoce, future Duke of Mangiloth, slept in his spotless chambers— dreaming of how to best frame and punish all who were doomed to cross his gloried path— here his father fought for years, with sharp and dirty sword, to keep the forces of King Sashara and Lycema at bay.

It is not often then that Rancoth and his son Thaegoce ever shared company. And because of this thin bond between father and son, when elderly battle-torn Rancoth finally returned to his capital of Valcoss, he did not look well upon his boy. He saw the truth of the situation which his wife Seclina could not: that their son was ridiculously horrid. On the night of his father's return, it is said that the only thing nine-year-old Thaegoce wanted to talk about was the manner of which his father slayed his enemies while on campaign. When Rancoth replied, it did not suffice for little Thaegoce. He desired to know details, and not just the details of the slayings, but the details of those who were damned— how they acted before death, what their words were and how they were said, how their bodies contorted down to the slightest squirm as a blade was drawn in.

Here, too, the marriage of Rancoth and Seclina was ruptured. Some wonder if the atrocity of Thaegoce was to blame for this rupture, and to them I say, you should not wonder, but know. Seclina was expelled from the palace of Valcoss, and Rancoth found a new wife down in Lycema, where the women were fair. Her name was Merfania, and apart from being far superior to Seclina in natural beauty, she was also of a genuine human countenance. She did not mind all that much to see a thing out of place, and did not strive for an impossible attaining of perfection as Seclina had.

It was not until 2216 that Rancoth arrived back in Valcoss with Merfania. Thaegoce had recently turned fourteen, and had just recently killed his mother.

For Seclina had been sent away to a brothel upon being stripped of her Duchess title years before, and no one now remembered her as anything more than a common beer man. Since Thaegoce had been attending brothels and inns since the age of twelve, forsaking his schooling for a more primitive form of learning, he had seen his mother many times, serving drinks to wermen in hardly any clothes, and this was no way for a son to see his mother. At first, Thaegoce simply enough opted to avoid his mother's residence, but after two years he realized that the image of his downcast bearer of life would not grant him peace, unless perhaps if the thought of her were to be snuffed away fully.

And so Thaegoce went to his mother's residence in disguise, with only his long, flowing, pure white hair cascading down from behind his mask. Even this would've been no indication to Seclina, who always had the hair of Thaegoce trimmed short and neat. And so, when Seclina received payment and a request from the strangely disguised voice in the strange costume, she accepted and they descended deep down spiraling step.

Thaegoce removed his mask immediately upon locking the door, so that this mother would know full well the terror of the situation she found herself in. Here was her son of sadism supreme, speaking to her on all the ways in which her methods had failed him. He spoke of an unhappy youth, wasted on vanity and manner, and led on by a mother who cared more for shining silver than the nature of lifelings. And he said it was fitting, then, that she should at last join her half of the race of men, here where they all belonged in the duchy of Mangiloth, in houses of pleasure. Thaegoce stuffed his mother's mouth with the excrement of sickly cows and then threw her into a deep basin— typically used for divine bathing rituals, but in this case, full of an odious mixture. There he bathed Seclina ferociously, bringing her head up often, not allowing her to die. For it has been stated on numerous occasion that the one true joy that Thaegoce received in life was that of pain, and so this night might have been akin to him what a craft fair might be to a child.

Departing from the death of Seclina, Lady of Mangiloth, we return to the day when Rancoth and his far younger wife Merfania rode into Valcoss. Thaegoce stood solemn in the window, the boy aged fourteen looking more like a statue than a living werman. But from the moment he caught glimpse of Merfania, he knew that he would endeavor to make her his own, and thus as well take from his father the second of his wives.

The seduction of Merfania appeared at first to be a joke, for the apparent difference in age. Thaegoce was fourteen; Merfania thirty-six. But Duke Rancoth had lost count of his own age once he had reached 75, and so Merfania realized that Thaegoce was in fact the closer of the two ages. She also began to realize that Rancoth was swiftly growing old, and would soon be immobile. Already was he a poor match in the bedchamber. And here where one might assume Thaegoce to be most inexperienced, he proved Merfania wrong. He put on a facade of gentleness, and rained down gold upon her as he suckled her extremities.

A plot was then devised to rip the duke Rancoth off his miserable course. It was simple enough, for Rancoth was a lover of pipe, and would smoke himself into slumber just short of alroads. One night then, when Merfania sat atop his chest— for Rancoth had been atop only once, on their first night and never again after— she blocked off the top of his pipe. She went on to shove it into his mouth, then quickly sealed the lips before accursed vomit made its way out. In this manner, Rancoth's lungs quickly filled with smoke, and Merfania fled the room. The sealing paste upon Rancoth's lips wore off, and when his corpse was discovered it was assumed that he simply choked upon his pipe.

And so Thaegoce rose to his seat of power with his father's widow as his bride. The duchy of Mangiloth was shocked to hear that the young duke was only aged fourteen, for his stature was quickly growing and he radiated strength and glory in his physique, as well as his perfectly straight and perfectly white hair. His harshened gaze also seemed advanced for his years; the peoples of Mangiloth thought it to be a look of wisdom and contemplation, though it would soon be discovered to simply be a look of heinous hatred and a love for nothing but suffering.

The first years of the reign of Thaegoce were spent traversing the territory of Mangiloth from east to west— from the capital of Valcoss to the more ancient town of Trosenia. Upon leaving, Thaegoce and Merfania brought behind them a train of 484 empty carriages, for they intended to fill each one of them. They filled them in the following manner: every four miles they traveled, they would stop at the nearest house. Whoever the unhappy soul inside may be, herim would receive a knock on the door, some well-intentioned greetings and banter, and then be informed that all their possessions were forfeit. If any objection was made, the unhappy soul would be shown the rotting corpse of a mutilated man, and then told that the loss of all worldly treasure is a kind gesture when put against a heinous loss of life and limb.

And in this way, going at only four miles a day, Thaegoce and Merfania trudged slowly across Mangiloth, looting relentlessly and filling their own carriages with as much glee as they could muster. But yet Thaegoce was never gleeful. The word does not suit him. Soon Merfania came to realize this, for being of the Lycemean breed she was well-humored and of playful stock. The depraved mind of her royal husband, then— though she found his physical splendor nothing short of attractive— was eventually too much for Merfania to bear. She sued for a parting of ways as they neared Trosenia, years after they had set out from Valcoss, perhaps now because there would be a well of fine wermen of power with whom she could now align herself in Mangiloth's second city.

But Thaegoce saw through the design of his lady Merfania, and years of companionship served as nothing to melt his iron heart. Upon arriving in Trosenia, he inspected his 484 carriages from their plunders along the road, and found one to be filled completely and to the brim with the soft and plush dolls that had been confiscated from little girls and boys. He suggested to Merfania that this would be a grand and heavenly place to make men for the last time, for a love affair as momentous as theirs had to be marked in some spectacular fashion. So into the carriage of dolls they went, where Thaegoce intoxicated Merfania, and in her sleep began to sew her into the combined fabric of a master doll. Many sedatives were needed to ensure a long sleep for the wife of Thaegoce, and indeed it took many days to perfectly design and execute the cuttings and sewings that would enable the doll carriage to become one singular thick and padded suit that would fit Merfania's body precisely.

When at last Merfania awoke, she found herself unbearably feverish, and when she opened her eyes saw nothing but darkness. She thrashed about, finding all her body inside a thick molding of doll-cloth, stuffed with a soft thickness all around. In the heat of the day, the interior of the costume was a roasting hell.

Thaegoce swiftly explained what he had done and what it was she found herself put inside, refusing her plea for release, and then swiftly threw her off a thousand-hand cliff, for genuine curiosity of whether she would survive or not.

For those unfamiliar with the geography of ancient Mangiloth — the place now residing in Ilandia— the cliff that Thaegoce threw Merfania from is known as The Rise. It is a steep drop, nearly straight down in fact, and it stretches straight across the land for many miles. On the high end of The Rise is the town of Trosenia, with the rumored locations of the Valley of Trosis lying shortly behind, and the bulk of Mangiloth stretching eastward. At the bottom lies a far desolation, stretching out in all directions, of lifeless and colorless land, among the most miserable and damning in all Elaptirius.

The Rise served as a great boundary in ancient times as an insurmountable barrier for those south and west who sought to discover what lie above. Additionally, the peoples of the Trosian Valleys were baffled at how to descend, and so for many ages primarily stayed close, for all ways around were equally perilous and falling down The Rise made for a certain demise. But not in this case.

Merfania was the first man that we know of to survive a fall from The Rise, and doubtless she survived only by the thick padding of her encasement. Thaegoce reached the bottom by way of a platform device, manned by a complex system of ropes, and approached the shaking mesh of fabric. Now he cut open the face of the doll, and saw the sweating convulsions of Merfania's broken face, barely clinging to life. Thaegoce had always intended this to be her end, and as she lay there dying, he caressed her cheek, whispering, "Do you remember what I told you on the night we met?"

Merfania could not find the strength to speak clearly, and so Thaegoce gave her the words. "I said that you looked delicious. Tastier than a Margwin pie."

And so he ate her.

There, in the dry plains beneath The Rise, beginning with the lips, he grasped tight with his teeth and ripped them off, then — well, I'm sure that's enough. He was a bad person. I believe we might all understand that after such tellings.

The encasing, drop, and feast of Merfania occurred in the year 2222, a year with many twos. Thereafter, Thaegoce advanced his tactics from that of domestic atrocities— that is, the quartering and looting of private homes— to widespread atrocities, mostly involving the burning of all towns in his path.

He took the legendary Chinjin Urier— that fabled warlord of the CLARFONATH who subdued half the continent far back in the Second Age— as a model, and in all ways imitating his beloved Chinjin Urier, Thaegoce roamed ahead an army of horsemen, weaving an unpredictable path of fire through not just Mangiloth but all the neighboring lands as well. Night raids were common, to the dismay of all, and the public blood-spilling of young girls brought forth sudden action from nations round the bout. A swift coalition was formed by three kings— Sashara of Lycema, Wythoon of Enceloth, and Bossum of Dikenia— to put a metal end to the Tyrant Duke of Mangiloth.

For years they chased Thaegoce to no end, across endless marsh and desert red, through Mistied Finger and Hollowed Round, and back and forth from the Andiloth more than a dozen times. Slowly the vast numbers of the coalition began to hack away at the swift though unskilled horsemen of Mangiloth, and when the coalition recruited foreign mercenaries, their combined forces were able to encircle the armies of Thaegoce and close down upon them.

The end— or, so it would seem— came fittingly enough at the ancient site of Yoren, the once central settlement of Chinjin Urier and his conquered lot. In this many-colored grassland, beset with stone ruins and enclosed by curved overarching hills, they slaughtered the last of Thaegoce's horseguard. Shocked they were, when victory had come, to find that none among them were Thaegoce. Certainly none could bear any semblance to the beautiful straight white hair for which he was famous. It seemed that the greatest enemy, he who had architected such death and destruction, had evaded the coalition despite all their long efforts. An unending watch was charged to all kingdoms within lettershot, and numerous bounties set upon the disgraced Duke of Mangiloth. The administration of the duchy was stripped to the bone and all

Mangilothian territories thereby split fairly between the kings of Enceloth, Lycema, and Dikenia. After years of silence, all assumed that Thaegoce was by then simply passed away.

On Ansila Siroth

In truth, Thaegoce had not simply passed away. The world would have grown merry again if he had, but then we would have no climax for this tale. For once the very real danger of the coalition hunting his head dawned upon him, Thaegoce fled south. He tore away from his horseguard in secret, and rode towards the fabled city of Ansila Siroth. Now, the city is here called fabled because in that time no one of any credibility had ever found it. Geographically speaking, it was quite easy to put on a map— south from the passes of Urvenhu, east from Thellig Rock, west from the Shilong Forest, north from the Deepest Pits— yet that is a broad hunk of land within those boundaries. And a labyrinth of dark and stony passes, curling this way and that, rising and falling among twisted obsidian towers, was enough to hinder the lame who ventured to seek it.

Thaegoce, however, was a noble duke, and the farthest from lame in his own mind. Therefore he ventured to seek Ansila Siroth with nothing but his own stunning physicality.

He could not find it.

He was lost among the winding maze for weeks, and he called out into the darkness with no response. His pure white hair grew littered with grime and dust, so that it was more brown than anything else, and seeing this drove Thaegoce to the brink of madness. At last, he ascended to the top of his path for the nineteenth time, which had no decent end, for it looked down only upon the Deepest Pits. But he could stand no more to wander about in worthless tracks that all led to bad ends.

So he screamed aloud and cursed the earth— making a firm point not to call upon any gods, for he did not believe in any— and cast himself down into the Deepest Pits. There, one can only pray that he met his demise, but woe to the world that such a drop was not terribly far, and this particular pit was filled with a bubbling mud. And so Thaegoce was dirtied once again, but did not die. He emerged laden in toxic filth, but once he climbed up from the pit he found no difficulty in making way towards the Longpis town of Lay Pork, on the southern border of the Pits.

In Lay Pork, Thaegoce persuaded the men of the Longpis— who had no affiliation with his adversarial coalition— to keep his location secret and to call for one of his armies to ride south. When his allies arrived, Thaegoce informed them that their home of Mangiloth was to be forgotten for now, as they would build a new regime in these unpopulated lands between Lay Pork and the Hollow Rounds, where no coalition would clash against them.

Again Thaegoce went searching for the fabled Ansila Siroth, and again he could not find it, not even with a troop of fifty men. So, frustrated, he set up citadel of his own as alternative. He called it Crissen, and it lay high upon a cragged rock between the labyrinth of obsidian towers and the Deepest Pits, not far off from where he had leaped in his hour of madness.

Once his citadel of Crissen was complete, Thaegoce did not leave for a span of nearly twenty years. I guess one might call him a recluse then. For in his black chamber he had a stunning view, looking westward over bloody red moonrises, the rolling Hills of Serco, the then-unnamed Wheat Fields and the town of Orpin Rude. It is here at his desk, overstretched with a boar's hide, that he would conduct correspondence with his captains and write out orders in his horrifyingly grotesque penmanship.

Quite often during the 2240s and 2250s, when Thaegoce resided unceasingly in the citadel of Crissen, he would have his captains deliver abducted girls to him, not for any sort of romantic purpose, but strictly for mutilation. Word spread and all within fifty miles were petrified of the storied Crissen, with none ever venturing eastward of Orpin Rude. A surprise indeed it was then, when Thaegoce looked out his window one eve to see three figures riding leisurely upon his black soils below. The central figure rode a white horse and wore a brown robe, ragged it seemed. Beside were two werman protectors, armored lightly but easily would they have been overcome by the numerous guards of Thaegoce.

Thaegoce emerged out of the door at the bottom of his great rock for the first time in nigh two decades. Such was his curiosity at the first willing visitors to his new land. "They say this is a dark place," spoke Thaegoce. "I do not believe that you have heard such speak, for if you had, surely you would be far from here."

The central figure removed her hood, showing herself to be none other than a bold and fiery woman, her eyes long with age yet her face young as ever, and her countenance with an unfearful, unchanging resolve. Her horse's hooves were planted firmly in the ground. And Thaegoce, who was known all the eastern world round for never breaking a stare, found this divine gaze too much to tolerate. As if struck by fire he snapped his face to one side.

Who it was that had ridden up to the stone citadel of Crissen on that night in nothing but a robe with two companions, was Melizar the Primordial— the same of the ancient Starlings who had done battle against Caldar of her own relation, and had sparked the first migration of Passians from Pendala down to Hayaman. She had kept quiet these last several hundred years, but still she endured, with none of her potency lost.

"I will be received as your finest guest tonight, Thaegoce of Mangiloth," she spoke calmly to the heinous recluse. "And you will find you are quite capable of providing hospitality, despite years of showing your captives anything but. For you will not harm me, but bow, for when you learn my name you will know that all your deeds amount to nothing when marked against mine."

And so Melizar went fearless up the tall black rock to the steel fortress of Crissen, where so many before had met an unforgiving doom, and she made herself quite at home, seating herself upon the fairest chairs of Thaegoce and sprawling out seductively. Thaegoce wanted nothing more than to take his blades to the perfect shape of her shining skins, for all that was beautiful he meant to mar in his time upon the earth. But he resisted the urge, for every word that came from Melizar's mouth was of pure grasp and command. She wielded such a knowledge of the world, and the tales of bygone hour, that it was impossible for any to deny her the time and heed she sought.

So she told all her story to Thaegoce, who watched on with the highest regard he had ever granted to any before. And all this time Melizar believed it was more than captivation that she caught in him— she believed that like all her conquests, he was enchanted under her spell of perfection. But after hearing all, and all told twice again, Thaegoce could speak his mind true and without filtering net.

"You speak of such power, but yet if mastery you hold above all, why is not all the world bowing before you this day? Why do you come to the hold of one whose reputation today dwarfs your own, with a host of only two and in a ragged robe, torn from years of disuse and spent wandering in deep woods of forgotten glory? You may have a great memory for the turning pages of the world but today you are weak. Yes, you are weak because you are indecisive. And you are indecisive because you do not know what you want. For instead of choosing, you simply want everything at once."

Here Melizar was the one stunned, for she had forgotten what it was to fail in casting a spell over wermen. Indeed, over the course of three thousand years, only a few handfuls of wermen had ever fallen short of submitting themselves to the fulfillment of her designs and desires, and her sway was almost just as predominant in women as well. But after the initial moments of surprise, Melizar began to realize that Thaegoce spoke true. By hearing the words of one who was so incredibly self centered as to not even be shaken by supreme beauty, she knew that his reason must be untampered and sound.

It was honesty and simple observation that compelled Thaegoce to point out the flaws in Melizar's designs, and she now took it to mind. She had been weak, and indecisive. For all her existence she had dealt on a moment's whim, never making scheme for anything grander than her present craving. Never making design for a plot that would shake the foundations of the earth and bring forth her glory for all the world. And so she resolved to design such a project in that instant, one that would consume her for the next three thousand years.

"I hear you, Thaegoce Whitestock, and I will now set my sights upon one single goal, from this day on, to create for the first time a position of ultimate mastery, to lord over all this land— not just these lands farthest from the rising sun, but all too stretching westward, to the far place they call Rocksend and down to the stormy mountains and seas past Alyinen, even south into the unknown regions of Gaelog. All will then hail me, for it will be law, even those seldom few who would not do so willingly, such as you."

Thaegoce let out a narrow smile at Melizar from his ill-preferred chair (Melizar occupied the better), one of the seven smiles that he ever made in his life. What he was thinking it would never be known, but surely in his dark heart he sought to use Melizar to a point and then cast her down before her designs of absolute mastery be realized. But he feigned admiration, and bowed humbly before this Primordial Starling. And from that point on Melizar took Thaegoce into her service, and Thaegoce took Melizar into his.

The first line of business in setting the Design of Absolute Mastery into motion was to acquire more forces, obviously. For at that precise moment in the year 2259 Thaegoce was still a wanted and hated man, despised for his crimes against all in his tenure as Duke of Mangiloth. And Melizar, thought by most to be nothing more than an old figure of legend, if proven genuine would be just as strongly hated. So instead of seeking to gain hold of the continent by means of political slithering, they endeavored first to turn what armies they could to their side.

Yonder in the Bloody Foreskins, west of Plains of Athuka and south of the tall Sashites, Caldar's ancient force of Stremianair soldiers roamed about as hunters, feasting upon the plentiful game in that region. Melizar sent Thaegoce out from Crissen to this wild westland— the first time he had left since the establishment of that citadel. So in The Foreskins then he cut off the wandering ranks of Caldar's Stremianair and turned them into what Melizar called Vexen Warriors— changing their nature not one degree but renaming them to signify a new age, and a new master of their order. For now they would serve Thaegoce, who presented himself as the second coming of Caldar. Or rather, the fourth coming, since Caldar had been imprisoned three times before, and was still held in a coffin beneath the waters of The Glimmer, unbeknownst to the Stremianair (now Vexen). And of course Thaegoce spoke nothing of Melizar, for the Stremianair had a long oral tradition and would not stand to serve the lifeling who unfairly defeated Caldar at their defining battle.

After the institution of the Vexen was anointed, Thaegoce bade them to spread outwards in a southerly direction, taking all they found into their cause. These lands south of Athuka belonged in my day to the nation of Ockland, though in the 2260s they would have been nothing more than a collection of primitive tribes, peaceful and therefore easily taken by the warlike forces descending upon them. This dozen-year time was for the collection and indoctrination of Melizar's forces— for they truly were under the command of the Great Evil Starling— though their figurehead was Thaegoce. It was Thaegoce that yelled out to them from high pedestal with inspired speeches of hatred, Thaegoce who walked through the ranks of inspections as the armies stood at attention, and Thaegoce what led them into the fabled city of Ansila Siroth, which was now opened to him.

Ansila Siroth was where the Vexen warriors were brought after three years of the strictest regime of preparation, during which many perished. If they survived and still swore loyalty to Thaegoce, they would march alongside him through the maze of black passes, then see rising above them a tall and narrow tower, spiraling up to a sharp needle of a peak. None were allowed to ascend the tower but Thaegoce himself, for in the highest chamber resided Melizar, who acted always from this place, unbeknownst to any below. Unbeknownst as well, was the forging of this force to all who dwelled in the civilized places north of the Gizle, for their concern was not with the barbarians of the south, and they noticed little that their peoples were being swept away, taken by a dark and rising power.

By 2271 then, Thaegoce had assembled a vast army in secret, staying hidden from the rest of the world in his guarded citadels of Crissen, and at the base of the towers of Ansila Siroth, which had grown large with Vexen camps. On the sixth night of Lurvarion he ascended the winding stairs of Melizar's tower, as he often did, though this night would not be like the others.

In her chamber, Melizar lay in a bath, golden and warm. Here she could look out on all sides at the dark country around her, for the chamber was open-air on all sides, but she looked instead upon her own hands, perfect and smooth. The only other in the chamber was Shiron, Melizar's most beloved servant from a time before Thaegoce. Shiron was a Pendalese werman, with enormous arms and a chest of near steel, with a solemn face of pure loyalty often hid by the nature of his attire. For he wore at almost all times a full suit of armor, polished with predominantly maroon set in with lines of gold. The armor was formed in connected curving sections, allowing for fluid movement and contraction. Even the helmet was such—extending directly up from the body and wrapping over all the head, not even leaving a slit for the eyes. In the coming war, all Melizar's Pendalese would don these suits of armor, and be referred to by the Angelons as the Maroons.

"You see that we are now close to obtaining our designs," spoke Melizar softly as white-haired Thaegoce entered in, feeling the warmth of the heated floor with the back of his hand. "Are you not pleased? Are you not enamored, with the vision you see before you now?" Thaegoce stared at Melizar in her bathing basin without a hint of emotion, for he truly laid claim to none.

Melizar rose, presenting her perfections to Thaegoce. "Do not continue to pretend, Lord Thaegoce. Long have you desired me, and I you, but we had much work to commit. Now we are twelve years on and the armies readied. Make rest for your troubles, and join me in this basin. We will rest here together."

But Thaegoce did not consent. "You believe that I have desired you by no skill of observation, for I have shown no signs. Rather you believe it because you believe you deserve the love of all men, as if it were your right to take it. Or perhaps because one like Shiron here has spent many years telling you exactly what it is you long to hear. But I am not Shiron. I am not one of the brown-skinned dogs of Pendala who cling to any who pass by who might seem more beautiful than the last. I am a golden-skinned heir to a kingdom"—

"A kingdom that was only just born," spoke Melizar as all the ways suddenly grew dark. "I was born to the kingdom of ancients, crafted by the very Lords of Margon who set this world into motion. And so I have come to give you my own gift: a body which shall not decay by means of age. But yet you mock me, when you should be praising my every word."

And here it is said that Melizar spoke for a good long while, but I do not wish to burden this work with an extra 35 pages. In short, Melizar disabled Thaegoce. Entirely so.

The first physical blow came unexpectedly, as Melizar signaled a trap door beneath the legs of Thaegoce. He then fell into the small chamber directly below— only tall enough to lie, and even then he was cramped. This little crevice beneath the floor was a furnace, run by real red flame, so installed that Melizar's chamber would have nice heated floors.

And so Thaegoce burned, mere inches beneath the feet of Melizar, who felt only a comfortable warmth rising up through her stone tiles.

Melizar did not intend for the figurehead of her armies to die in this instance— she was too clever for that. And so she pulled him out before the life was suckled out, and dug in her claws. Many things she tore out, many things she pulled, and many things did she bite on with ravishing wrath before the main order of business was to be carried out.

She stuck Thaegoce with a series of hooks—- thousands of hooks— sharp hooks with bent tips; stuck them in far and then pulled them out, though they were in his body for good due to the nature of the deep bent blades. And then with all of the body punctured, Melizar wrapped him round with the thin wires that proceeded the hooks. She pulled upon the wires, hard so that the body of Thaegoce was nearly sliced into ten-thousand bits in an instant. She stopped a moment when the wires were tight, tight enough to keep him from squirming a single inch. And then Melizar brought down her hammer, battering in the wires and smashing Thaegoce into an eternal submission.

For three years Melizar pummeled the body of the once-duke of Mangiloth, whose spirit it is said did not flee the body only for the reason that hatred is an earthbound thing, and a man fueled completely by such is destined to never return to lands before or after the world. Deep into the year 2274, Melizar had at last constructed a vile contraption to encase her greatest slave, and here was the transition that turned the worldly Thaegoce into the symbol of true horror that has come down to us through the haunts of history.

"You are Thaegoce no more," spoke Melizar, "but rather now you shall be called Haegos, a terrible sounding name for a wretched creature who will stalk the earth for ages to come. And just as you have spent your days dominating the lives of men, now so shall I dominate you, and abuse you to my will."

And so she truly came to take Haegos into her service, enchanting his steps and having him move with dread wherever she pleased. The Vexen at the base of Ansila Siroth had waited patiently— a long thousand days— for their leader to return to them. And when he at last emerged out of the tower a striking figure of black metal dread, they had no doubts that this was their captain. They cheered as Haegos displayed his terrifying might, taking off the heads of several who stood in the front ranks, and holding them up by their necks.

Meanwhile, Melizar stood in the shadows of her high chamber, still unknown to the armies she would now lead through the puppet Haegos. As she looked towards the west she could see a burning white sun rising. It was time for the war to begin.

On Wilderfrant VII, or The Young King

And this takes us back to 2275, at the moment of Old King Wilderfrant first hearing the name Haegos, and first coming to realize that he might not so easily live out all his long years without some sort of fight. Violence was not a thing he opted for, but his son implored him to meet the enemy while they were still far out of reach of Angelon. This, the fact they were still far out of reach, the Old King pushed as reason to simply stay out of the affairs of others. But the young Wilderfrant VII had just recently been crowned as monarch alongside his father, and now had his own voice to be heard.

"Better to see what is out there before it arrives on our doorstep. If there is any truth to these reports, then this is not a thing to be brushed aside," spoke the Young King.

The Old King grumbled. The coronation of his son in his own lifetime was meant to be something altogether new and exciting. For the first time in the history of that great realm, two kings would rule at once. But now that a matter of pressing urgency presented itself, the Old King found himself remorseful that he now held only half the power of the crown.

The decision ultimately landed upon Stindard Lewd, the long-held advisor to the Old King. May it be said that the Lewds are of a golden hue— even more so than the golden hue that Thaegoce always claimed to have— and with faces that hold an expression of extreme wisdom, and capable of switching instantly to an expression of extreme silliness. Both these countenances they are unrivaled in by all the peoples of the earth.

Now, Stindard Lewd granted credence to both sides of the argument. Never one to disagree with his lord and master The Old King, whom he had served loyally for half a century, he found it truly unsettling to speak his mind. Yet he was compelled to do so:

"If you will remember forty years behind, my lord, to a time when our allies fought against Thaegoce of Mangiloth. This great nation was absent in the fight, and how has this generation viewed us for it? We are left out of that page of history, and rightfully so, for while your father and later yourself could have put forth valiant effort alongside our sister nations, you chose the path of shame and indignity. Now here is a chance to redeem your good name— to show the young of our kingdom that Old King Wilderfrant was not so idle as to pass up two wars in his lifetime. Every great lord has his fight, and you've yet to have yours. So I side with your boy. We must ride to meet this new threat. We must do so if only to put right what is now past."

And so in saying this, Stindard Lewd sealed his own fate, as well as the fate of the Kingdom of Angelon. By the end of a fortnight, the king's forces were readied and began the march south, to do battle with Haegos.

The first great battle in that long and vile war was that of the Orpin Rude. The location was determined by the Old King, who was shown a sprawling map of the lands near Haegos' stronghold and advised that the high pass over Orpin Rude would be an ideal place to strike, for it commanded a wide vista over the open road below.

And so Wilderfrant VI sent out emissaries to Haegos' camp at Crissen, to declare a state of hostilities and invite them to open battle upon the plains of the Orpin Rude, himself planning to command a secret division of men from the high pass. His son Wilderfrant VII objected, saying that an enemy told to be so cunning would surely suspect such a ruse, and would themselves fashion a countermove to buckle the legs of the Angelon army. But the Old King placed full faith in his forces, being as the Angelons were as yet undefeated in battle since the founding of their kingdom.

At dawn on the last day of Wethember, in the recorded 2275th year, soldiers began to rise in their camps outside the town of Orpin Rude. The small white cliffs studded with green proved a calming morning sight, and victory felt assured, for to their backs— upon the high pass— grey-aged Wilderfrant VI hid just back from the cliffside, ready to come forth with three masses of archers as soon as the enemy rushed on.

As the sky erupted with the sound of battle horns and the first charges commenced, the Old King— surrounded by the likes of his son, Stindard Lewd, and Stindard the Younger— trotted forward upon his horse, and gave the command for the first row of archers to move for the cliffside. There, they readied their bows and delivered a fierce volley to the charging enemies below. The wave of arrows knocked down many of the Vexen warriors to the ground, but their armor was thick, and thus few of their lives were broken. As the first line of archers lowered themselves, reaching for their arrows, the second line rose up and delivered their volley. It seemed to be the perfect strategy, for their place on the high ground was firm and their archers precise. Yet the Vexen were too swift, and the arrows hindered them only slightly in a short delay.

Minutes after the charge, the two armies on the plain clashed in a fierce melee. The Angelons on the ground had not expected a direct conflict of such ferocity, being told that the archers on the ridge would resolve the conflict before it came to blows. But it was not so. And even as things began to look dreary— for how now could the archers fire into the clash with hopes of killing the Vexen but not their own men?— suddenly matters grew far more hopeless. A secret army of Haegos began a charge from behind the Old King Wilderfrant, on the high pass. And this was no mere army of men, but of Desiroth. These were the many descendants of the ancient Passians of the Second Age who were taken by Caldar and crafted into grotesque beings of beast-like quality, and all took surprise at their sudden coming. For this race of being had not been seen for many hundreds of years, and even as the armies of Haegos grew, their existence was kept secret. It was here at the First Battle that they were to be unveiled, and their unveiling proved too much for the king.

As the hideous Desiroth came ever closer, just barely being held off by the back row of archers, Wilderfrant VI became short of breath. He gasped, hiccuped, gurgled in his throat as if something had become caught. And then from the plains below a new terror was flung upon them: the entrails of their slaughtered men. The Vexen were using trebuchets to launch the inners of the dead upon the archers on the high pass, and this brought the Old King to a faint.

Stindard Lewd cried out that the king was brought down and needed to be brought away from the battle immediately, so he and his son Stindard the Younger carried the Old King— coming in and out of consciousness— away to safety. Moments after setting Wilderfrant in his carriage, Stindard Lewd was shot through the ass, with a stray arrow.

"It's fine, Father," lamented Stindard the Younger. "Many a man have lived out the remainder of their days without asses. You will live!"

But Stindard shook his head. "This arrow has come upon me from the side, and in doing so has pierced the left cheek and gone right through to the right. The cheeks of my ass are therefore brought together, now at the end, and I pass on feeling a warm sensation that the space between had prevented all throughout the whole of my long life."

And there Stindard Lewd fell, accepting of his fate, and with a long arrow pushing the cheeks of his ass together at last.

Elsewhere, the volleys of entrails had turned to volleys of worms. Not the kind of small worms that one might find in the earth, but Ansilian worms— therefore being long and thick, with faces of their own— and so resembling the thinly sliced guts that had come before. The archers atop the ridge were at first unaware that the shots had changed. When the supposed entrails begin wiggling around, the archers believed themselves to have gone mad in the heat of the bloody battle. But soon they realized that no longer were guts being fired at them— those they had come to handle— but rather these were live chunks of giant creepers, who would stick onto the body and work their way to the backside if not killed soon enough.

Seeing that victory was at all odds unattainable, and the complete destruction of the army inevitable, Young King Wilderfrant ordered an immediate retreat. Those fighting on the plain made their escape whatever way they could, while the remaining archers on the ridge stood their ground as the Vexen now began to run up the cliff to finish them. Stuck between raging Desiroth behind and the incomprehensible skill of the

Vexen scaling the cliff, the archers had nowhere to go. And so they fired arrows to the last, until being swept off the pass.

The first battle of the Haegosian War had been a disaster. Not the worst disaster the men of Angelon would face in those years, but an unexpected disaster that they had not anticipated. However, three of every five men returned to Angelon Othim after the fight. That is not to say that they all went on with their lives— for of that number, another half was wiped out by a sudden sickness that was caused by the Ansilian worms. For unbeknownst to most, the worms had dug into their anal tubes, and there began to wreak havoc upon the body. Women spit up green. Wermen pissed out black. And an oozy blue was turned the skin of all of them.

In this way, the sickness of worms came to claim more lives of the Orpin Rude soldiers than the battle itself. To counter the devastating sickness, Young King Wilderfrant— now acting king, for his father remained in a long sleep— brought a new lead physician down from Medredum in Pendala. His name was Andito Mallurd, and he would serve the peoples of Angelon well until an unfortunate incident that we will yet come to.

In the after days of Orpin Rude, long councils were convened and argued. Eventually, it was the decision of the Young King to sue for peace, and declare the lands already then lost to Haegos as forfeit. He could not afford to cook together a new army, for his was now obliterated by battle, sickness, and desertion. There then seemed to be no other option.

And so time hurried on in a state of lingering dread, quiet yet every hour filled with the silent crack of approaching doom. All the while the Old King lie in bed, the horrors of Orpin Rude keeping his eyes shut to the world. For just shy of two years did he remain in an unwakable sleep, confounding Andito Mallurd and the traveling physicians of his day. Yet still the king breathed, as though in gentle slumber, and so he was attended to at all hours unto his waking, which came in the middle of the year 2277, on the eleventh of Sexarion.

"You've slept just shy of two years," fingered Stindard the Younger as the king at last opened his eyes. "You should feel refreshed beyond the power of age."

And for a moment the Old King was. "And I suppose you've spent all of those two years right there watching me like an eyelid-less bird," he muttered with a smirk, but soon enough dark thoughts overtook him once more, just as they had on the high pass of Orpin Rude, just before he fell into his long sleep. But Stindard the Younger assured the elderly monarch that those evil days were done. The armies of Haegos had stopped on their course, and were summarily defeated. Of course it was a lie, but it needed to be said if the Old King was ever to rise from his bed.

Days later, Wilderfrant VI finally got up the strength to walk out into the sun. He was greeted by applauding citizens in his courtyard, and he smiled as he held up his wrinkled hand. But as gazed round, his eyes stopped on a black blot. There was a dark wave moving on the horizon, just outside the city. Soon the peoples in the courtyard began to take notice as well, running about for their homes. The Old King felt faint once again, but was caught by Stindard before he fell.

"What is this?" Weakly asked the Old King. "Defeated are they? And how many times has this city been under siege while I slept? You are no son of your father, now tell me where is my son, so that I might once more hear the ring of truth in my ears."

At that precise moment, Young King Wilderfrant was in fact riding out from the city on a lightning steed, with a host of the fastest riders in the kingdom, to meet the rapidly approaching Desiroth force head on. They had been sent out quietly, for Stindard had calculated the size of the encroaching threat and thought it could be easily dealt with, and so did not desire alarm for the people, least of all the newly-awakened elder king.

But such a strategy proved faulty. For already spies of Haegos had penetrated the city, coming in small numbers over the course of the last year and acting no stranger than any of the other folk. This then would explain the massive surge in population that had occurred in those months— which Wilderfrant VII had shown concern for, but was dissuaded by Stindard from taking action.

So on this day all the city of Angelon Othim was brought to war. It had arrived without ever there being a siege, and with the experienced men far out from the gates. It was to the local craftsmen and vendors then that this burden of battle fell: the mothers and the fathers, the children who found their wits, and the great bears who were at all times kept in the Old King's hall— now in this dire hour set loose.

Horns were sounded as soon as they could be reached, for the Young King and his riders to turn back immediately and defend the city. But by that time, those forces were already in thick, and found it hard to break away with tens of Desiroth scrambling about each man.

On into the evening the streets sounded out with the hiss of scraping metal, and structures caught fire at an increasing rate. The city then was evacuated, and those who could escape fled swiftly in a westerly direction. As twilight began to approach, the gates of the city were battered down by a fresh march; this time it was the maroon-armored Pendalese, led by Shiron, the well-trusted servant of Melizar. Though one could never tell any of these warriors apart in their full-bodied armor. Anyway, they brought the real thunder of death. With their long curved swords, sectioned so as to have five separate hooks on the blade, the Maroons brought swift ruin to even the skilled of the city's soldiers.

Wilderfrant VII and Stindard the Younger fought side by side, fiercely in the dying hours of daylight. With roars, grunts, and faces dirtied with ash and blood, they held a narrow passage leading towards the king's hall against the ancient Desiroth. But as the Maroon approached they knew they'd soon be in for a crushing. For the Maroons marched slowly, assured in their victory, and inspired fear by their tall stance and shining armor alone. True enough, Stindard the Younger fell after mere moments battling one of these, being pierced straight through the stomach and out the spine. How, in those few cold moments before death, he longed for his father's arrow through the flaps of ass.

As the murderous Maroon removed her blade, Stindard fell backwards to the ground and the Young King sprinted back towards the king's hall, to protect his father. But he was not timely. For as Young Wilderfrant bolted through the gates, he saw first a family of bears ripping folk to chunk, and then out upon a bridge he glimpsed his father. With his bow he fired nine arrows at the escaping Desiroth who held him, but Wilderfrant VII was notoriously not of good aim and none of the arrows made their mark.

The elderly king was then dragged out of the city by heinous foe. Already limbs were ripped from his body before he reached the edge of Angelon Othim, for kingly limbs were later found along a course leading from the bridge to the gates. Then, outside the city, he was summarily executed. Details are not necessary to describe the vile killing of a royal figure hardly able to stand, but let it suffice to say that the forces of Haegos were not gentle about his body.

Some who remained in the city were able to hide in dark places over the course of the starless night. Young King Wilderfrant— now the sole King Wilderfrant— was one of these, as he sat silently in a rat cupboard while Desiroth, Pendalese Maroon, and filthy spy alike had a celebratory beer, which lasted twelve hours. At last he made his escape at noon, when all the city was quiet with the sounds of evil things taking their rest.

As he departed Angelon Othim, Wilderfrant VII saw the phrase "Formoss Mali Kor" vandalized at least thirty-nine times. This in the Sheelkonti Tongue means "Death to Kings," and was the rallying cry of Haegos and his armies. As Wilderfrant snuck out of his capital, he even caught glimpse of Haegos himself, wandering the streets, appearing to be of an aimless mind. But as the new lord of cruelty looked up, revealing his spiked helmet of dread, Wilderfrant knew this truly was a figure to be feared. But though afraid, he knew that he would continue to fight this demon until his final breath. And with this thought in his head, away he fled.

The Battle of Angelon Othim had brought about the First Migration of the Angelon peoples. For they could not inhabit an overrun capital. And so they put up a new temporary capital in Frawlin, to the west, on the north bank of the Andiloth. Frawlin was the third city of Angelon, after Lucilian, but Lucilian lay to the east and therefore had a stronger chance of also being overrun by Haegos.

Frawlin, in many regards, was a nicer spot for a capital anyway. It lay for the most part hidden among fine woods— the green kind that one did not see much on the east side of Denderrin Othim. People of a nasty humor would sometimes joke that it was a blessing that Haegos had ripped the first capital out from under them. But Wilderfrant was in no mood for jokes in the year following 2277. He was hard with work, building his army anew. One that would stand and not be disbanded nor defeated amidst the raging tides of Haegos.

The first of the allies Wilderfrant VII summoned to his court was an old friend from childhood— perhaps his first friend— Wythoon II of Enceloth. Wythoon had been king in his own right for almost nine years now, and was five or so years older than Wilderfrant, so the exiled King of Angelon looked to him as a figure of wisdom, despite them both only being in their twenties. Their first meeting after six years was one of pure joy, and possibly the only night of pure joy that Wilderfrant felt in his time at the Frawlin court.

"Do you remember that barrel of crispened milk chunks we ate when we were children?" Asked Wilderfrant, remembering fondly.

"It would have been an impressive feat for grown men," laughed Wythoon. "But we were busy with a battle of our own that day, and needed the sustenance."

"Yes, battling all the armies of Caldar in the West, how could one forget. And just as we obliterated those fictitious boyhood armies off the strength of nothing but milk chunks, so shall we deal with Haegos and his lot."

The second man that Wilderfrant allied himself with was the lovely King Sashara of the woman-kingdom Lycema, now 88 years old but still breathtakingly beautiful.

"I see at least your country has joined these conflicts," spoke Sashara, hinting that if Wilderfrant acted right he might yet find his way into the chamber of the storied queen at last on that night. "What took you so long? For as you know, my nation of Lycema fought hard the man called Thaegoce many moons past, while your father sat forever on his throne, diddling dog paws."

"I apologize, High King of Lycema, but I am not my father. I am displeased to say he was taken by the Desiroth, carried outside our city walls and dismembered. But as king of these exiled peoples I will not rest until our home is taken back."

Whether or not Wilderfrant made it into that holiest of royal chambers upon that night, I will leave for the reader to decide.

The third ally that Wilderfrant sought was the new lord from the southern land of the Longpis. He was Hipfinger, and this first of many Hipfingers holds the honor of being the first recorded fat man in all of Denderrin Othim.

"You are fat," spoke Wythoon as Hipfinger entered into the court of Frawlin for the first time.

Hipfinger jollied along, pointing a big finger at Wythoon— "It is true I be more akin to the bear than the goat, but I will not be long alone. For my stature declares to the world that I am well-moneyed and well-fed. In the coming years I believe a great many folk will begin to fatten their balls, for it makes me wise and homely to be large."

"Maybe so, but this is a council of war," argued Wythoon. "How will you ride a horse? How will you lift a sword? Of course I am only jesting, but in a way I'm not at all. For these villains are the most heinous our land has ever seen. And I have a great fear that you will be mowed down instantaneous if you ride out in that condition."

"Then my son Vilan will take my place as Noble Lord of the Longpis Realm!"

And that's exactly what happened.

For when the new Wilderfrantian Coalition was ready, they rode out in the year 2279 to chase the armies of Haegos from Angelon Othim and back into their southerly place of origin. For many weeks the campaign went smoothly, with the Coalition pursuing the Desiroth across the Flatrocks and the Red Canyons, where re-enforcements from Lycema and a fresh army from Dikenia joined the smiling 23-year-old king. The hunt then veered south. Chasing the enemy over the Hills of Serco, at last Wilderfrant saw the thing he dreaded most: a full army of Haegos, stood firm in front of him, with Pendalese Maroons comprising the front lines. Here there would be another merciless battle, the Third in the long War of Haegos.

"We must turn back!" Advised Wythoon, who rode always to the right side of Wilderfrant. "We have ridden hard this day and did not expect this. If we fight we will be beaten."

There was little time for contemplation. There stood the enemy in the bright daylight, not a mile away, and to many appearing to be unvanquishable. Yet something spoke to Wilderfrant in that moment. Something, some might argue, that came from a deep recess of the heart which is only listened to in the most deranged of circumstances. Deranged, then, must Wilderfrant have been, for he cried aloud his desire to attack:

"Let us not be fearful this day! The length of four long years has this rival haunted us; let us now show our vengeance, and bid them a hellish voyage to the suns where all the damned lie in eternal anguish! Do this today!"

"But have we any strategy at all?" Yelled the sweating Hipfinger.

King Wilderfrant turned to face forward upon his steed and whispered assuredly to himself, "Our strategy is to charge." And so they did.

Now, let it be said that on a rare occasion, an act of supreme folly may end in some unexpected good. Mainly, it will end as a farce with a spreading of cheeks. But this day— the fifth of Nanethis, 2279— proved to be one of truly few and sparse times when a foolish decision led to nothing but glory. For Wilderfrant and his coalition won the day in the Battle of the Wheat Fields, and the basic happening of things is laid out below.

The initial charge was in fact a disaster. The Maroons stood firm, as they always did, and the front lines of Wilderfrant were smashed against an unbreakable wall of armor. But veer then did the king and his line of nobility, ranging around the Haegosian block. The true blessing of the day was the horse, which all in the Angelon force rode, and the fact that many standing for the enemy did not. They were then unable to strike Wilderfrant's men with spear or arrow, for too swift did they prance, running in unstraight paths to make the task of the enemy even more trying. When the fight moved into the tall golden wheat and the Vexen pursued on foot, they quickly grew exhausted in the heat of the burning season, and lagged greatly behind. Far ahead then on the backs of their hoofed friends, the armies of Wilderfrant turned and made second charge. This proved much more effective, for there were great spaces between the Vexen now and they flew up with the cleaving of a sword, then down with fatal slices.

There was in the Haegosian army one troop of Maroon riders, which posed the greatest threat to Wilderfrant and company. These charged like lions, and hurled sharp javelins at the Angelons, succeeding in de-horsing many. Hipfinger of the Longpis was one such easy target, and he himself was among the first to be unhorsed. His horse Befilla was killed by the spear strike and would not rise again. And so Hipfinger cried aloud for one of the nobility to ride near to him, so that he might be brought back up onto the safety of a beastback.

But his yells and huffs gave signal to the Maroons— who relied on their ears to guide them for their armor covered the eyes— and a pack of them rode directly to the Longpis Lord. As fast as he could did Hipfinger run, but he was slow and jiggly in the race. His sweating grunts betrayed him, and a spear from a

Maroon was propelled right through the back of his neck. Thus was the passing of Hipfinger the First. Within a week of the battle, minstrels of Angelon came to compose "Lament for Hipfinger"— it is among the saddest of songs ever written.

Many wept mid-fight to lose a lord so great. But Wilderfrant inspired them again to great and heroic deeds, and so the day turned once more glad. The true victor of that battle would come to be fire. For the Angelon horses had been trained to ride in leaps when flame was at hand, and with the slaying of Hipfinger, the time for flame was certainly at hand.

At first, only a few torches were lit by the most eager of the Longpis crowd, and they were condemned by the Lycemeans for their stupidity. But their stupidity in lighting a fire which consume all the fields came to rule the fate of the hour. For as a blazing inferno swept across all the wheat, so the enemy was overwhelmed. The Maroons who put all trust in their sharp ears were at a loss, for the peaceful golden land was at once turned to a haven of indiscernible screams from all directions. The gold turned to red and black as evening took on. And though the armor of the Maroons could hardly be pierced, they were easily knocked to the ground by heavy swords of the Angelons, and left their to suffocate and burn as Wilderfrant's men raced swiftly on beastback.

A thousand times on that day a man from the Angelon forces imagined that herim had dealt the knocking blow to Shiron, leader of the Pendalese Maroons. For it was easily imagined, being there was no way to tell them apart through their armor. But in truth, none of them had succeeding in dealing this blow, for Shiron himself was not present. He was stationed to the east, in the Deepest Pits, and soon received word that his army had been decimated. Off to Ansila Siroth then did Shiron hasten back, to receive due punishment from Melizar and the new list of command. The garrisons were pulled out of the conquered cities to the north and brought back to the seats of power at Ansila and Crissen, giving their numbers time again to rise; such was the disastrous blow to the forces of Haegos and Melizar in the Wilderfrant Wheat Fields— newly named by the proud king himself, citing his great victory as cause for the place to bear his honor.

And so for a time things appeared to have regained their beauty, and it was believed that Haegos was only a passing shadow that had loomed large for four years and would now be extinguished. Wilderfrant VII— or Wilderfrant the Glorious, as he was now called by some— and Wythoon led their armies back into Angelon Othim, a ruined city of charred stone and littered street. But they set to work and soon it resembled its former cleanliness, though it never regained its position as the capital of the realm. For the vast sum of folk had found comfort in Frawlin, and were ill at ease about returning to a city where the memory of evil things still dwelt. Angelon Othim, then, was occupied by the king's forces in these years, as an eternal watchtower to lands on all sides, and a stronghold of their military might.

After the retaking of Angelon Othim, Wilderfrant returned to Frawlin with assured confidence. He had spent the last four years in utter fear and solemnity, but on this night he could at last smile and take notice of the freshness in the air. He was told it would soon be time to marry, and being presently filled with joy— and not knowing when joy might again depart— he decided to choose his bride on that night. For the breeze was soft and the trees of sweet aroma, with the moon bright and full, and the sound of heavenly horps sounding out in the halls. It was then that Wilderfrant chose his wife in the most peculiar way.

He arranged for all the women in the city line down and fart aloud, and then shit in bulk. The lady with both the loudest fart and shit of the highest bulk would then rise up as Queen of Angelon. As it happened, the winner of the contest chanced to be of displeasing structure, and so quietly Wilderfrant amended the contest so that the second champion would be the true champion, and he feigned that this was the intention all along to save the first champion from embarrassment. Within the hour, Wilderfrant was married to this woman with both the second loudest fart and second high bulk of shit in all of Frawlin. And her name was Emilorthan.

The 2280s were, for the most, part quiet. The war did continue after some years of Haegos rebuilding his forces, but it was continued by means of raids, siegecraft, and long uneventful chases. Strongholds were held, cities fell back and forth, but nothing of decisive consequence occurred. In the ensuing years, the enemy was held at bay by Witlonk the Firespear, tireless captain of the constant raids against the advancing forces of Haegos.

In 2290, Young King Wilderfrant— who was now himself 34 years aged— gave birth to his first child. He rather disliked the sensation of it, as have most who have ever endured childbirth, and so his remaining three offspring would all be born through the body of his queen. But pleased he was at the outcome of the birth, a vibrant child who would be yet another Wilderfrant. It was getting ridiculous at this point. To have eight kings in a row named Wilderfrant. And this eighth consecutive Wilderfrant realized it early on, and so opted to be called Erfrant, just for the sake of variety. But we cannot indulge in Erfrant's adolescence quite yet, for a major event is yet to be covered.

2291 brought the Fourth Great Battle between the Kingdom of Angelon and the dread forces of Haegos. It was fought at or around Thellig Rock, but that is all we know, for no chroniclers rode with the soldiers to that fight. Indeed, even if they had, it is doubtful any would have came back to share the tale, for of the five thousand that rode out from Angelon Othim, nigh of twenty ever found their way back to the city, many of which crawling or dismembered, or of serious disillusion. When questioned afterwards on their accounts of the battle, none of the survivors would speak on the subject. It is assumed that all others who gave fight to the enemy were either captured or killed.

The Battle of Thellig Rock, then, was a failure.

At least part or perhaps all of the extent of this failure was due to the Archangel of Cathuma, Caldar's ancient beast of unnatural birth, with horror etched into his existence from the start. The Archangel was recently discovered hidden in the West, and was now a new addition to the Ansilian army. He was first seen standing atop Thellig Rock in 2289— a symbolic seat that made clear the Archangel's intention to topple the very foundations of the kingdom. It was Witlonk Firespear who brought back this first report from one of his raids, and he described the Archangel as cloaked all in black robes which fluttered violently in the wind yet never showed face nor limb. Iron spikes wrapped around the extremities and shot up the back, giving the appearance of a dark throne, but appearing to support the otherwise unstable steps of the curious imposing figure. Twice the size of a man it was, for when it stood next to its Vexen captains they would come but to the waist.

The course of the year did not lighten after the calamity at Thellig Rock. For shortly thereafter, bolstered by their show of strength, the enemy raced up the Curved Road to Angelon Othim. The endless flood of Vexen and Desiroth would have been easily enough to snatch the city back from the Angelon soldiers there stationed, but the Archangel of Cathuma escorted them regardless. And great slaughter did he bring. For Wythoon of Enceloth was slain in a most unholy manner, in front of his child friend King Wilderfrant.

It happened so: with agile hands Wythoon dealt blows to the Archangel, whose gloved hands seemed impossibly large. As one would later learn, they were not hands at all, but rather— well, we will come to that in due time. But after a valiant fight, the Archangel took his swordless hand and lunged it at Wythoon, grabbing his head and sucking it inside the sleeve of its cloak. A few confused moments ensued, filled with an all-too-loud sound of grinding metals, and then all gasped to see Wythoon's head fall from the sleeve of the Archangel, all from the neck up razed to the bone. King Wilderfrant was only spared by his immediate leap into a sewage pipe, which proved too small for the Archangel of Cathuma. Angelon Othim, then, was taken again, and here would begin the Second Exile in the wars of Haegos.

After the crushing defeats of 2291, as well as the death of Witlonk Firespear and the majority of his company in a failed upon Urna Noht, it became apparent that— in the coming years— it would be up to a new rising generation to reclaim the lands lost to Haegos. Future hopes now rested on such names as Peril of Enceloth, Jasper of Dikenia, and Trilsenya of Lycema— all mere infants at the time but all heirs to kingdoms that could sway the winds of the war. And indeed for better or worse— and in some cases both— all of them would come to carry great impact.

One might wonder why I choose to leave out the young prince Erfrant, who was born in 2290 to the beloved Wilderfrant VII, from the prior list. To speak plainly, it is because the young man who was destined to be Wilderfrant VIII showed little prospect early on for any type of military tact. He had talents elsewhere, and there is where he devoted his energies.

For example, the young prince was far fonder of music than any of his kin. He was a master of both the furdle and the sloot. He also took a liking to plays and writing, and even a touch of philosophy. Strange attributes for a king, thought all within earshot of the Angelon court. But still King Wilderfrant played the role of designation, and pushed his son Erfrant towards an unwilling friendship with Peril of Enceloth. For Peril was the son of Wythoon, Wilderfrant's boyhood companion, and he missed his friend dearly after witnessing his death at the hands of the Archangel of Cathuma. Crafting a friendship between Peril and Erfrant akin to his own was the only thing that seemed right to Wilderfrant in a world where his friend had been so mercilessly taken from him.

Evidence for Wilderfrant's push can be seen in the year 2300, when the allied nations of Angelon, Enceloth, Lycema and Dikenia were all held in a long council at Arthconendin on the borders of what is now Piglandium, a location kept secret from all but those in attendance. There, as the fastly aging adults discussed the serious matters, the highborn children of the realms played in a less serious manner, though very much under the constant supervision of their respective households.

There was Trilsenya of Lycema, sixteen year-old daughter to King Lycef, who we have not yet mentioned. And indeed Lycef does not figure into any extant poems or songs of her time, even in her own country, and so one must presume that she was utterly insignificant. But this Trilsenya was already taking after her great-grandmother Sashara in more ways than one, and fate would have her live a long long life of wisdom, beauty and fairness.

There was Trilsenya's brother Elstone, aged twelve, who proved a more suitable friend to ten year-old Erfrant than did Peril of Enceloth, despite the wishes of King Wilderfrant, who longed to see his own boyhood friendship with Wythoon rekindled through their children.

Also among the children at Arthconendin was King Wilderfrant's second son, Himgo. He was not yet five years old at the time, and so while the other youthlings sat around wooded stone and discussed their version of politics, young Himgo was left out and harassed— for being five, he was not yet able to hold speak with the more sophisticated words that those of the age ten or twelve are used to using. But the joke would be put to their butts in due time, for Himgo was to impregnate his first lass at the age of thirteen, some well years before any of the rest. And this child of Himgo would be the one to carry on the line of kings in DANE, but we have not gotten far ahead of ourselves.

The last of the royal children who played in the woods outside Arthconendin in the vexing year of 2300 was Jasper of Dikenia. Here will begin a new chapter, for the character of Jasper would prove to be more pivotal than one might expect, and his memoirs linger long on the days at Arthconendin; indeed if it were not for those writings, we would know little of the relationships that begin in those early days.

On Jasper

Of the six aforementioned highborn children who found themselves at Arthconendin in the year 2300— Erfrant, Himgo, Trilsenya, Elstone, Peril and Jasper— four of them would meet grisly fates all upon the same night, 23 years later. That can be simplified into saying that two out of each three, would meet grisly fates upon the same night 23 years later. And the reason for that lies chiefly upon the werman whose name lines this chapter.

Jasper rode into Arthconendin in a blue carriage. He was clean and well-groomed, with a long and straight crop of hair flowing down past his shoulders, in all ways like that of Thaegoce except for it was pure black instead of pure white. Stepping down out of the carriage, young Jasper bowed before King Wilderfrant VII of Angelon and his household. Wilderfrant kissed Jasper's mother— reigning king of Dikenia — upon the cheek and then took swift opportunity to introduce the boy to his own, standing by politely.

"This is my boy, the eighth of the Wilderfolk. Though he likes to be called 'Erfrant.' Says it should avoid confusion. I don't know about that! But it'll do for a pet name til the day he'll come to take my throne out from under my rotting corpse. Anywhat, there's only two years between so you little wermen should get on fine."

He patted the young prince of Dikenia on the back and set him along. "I saw you rode up in a blue carriage," quietly spoke the timid Erfrant. "Blue is my favorite color."

Jasper took one glance at Erfrant's outfit and gave full critique. "I could've assumed as much as you're dressed in nothing but. You know, if you desire to make a color pop, you need to have it contrasted with others— drowning out our eyes with blue does nothing but annoy us with it. I take it you're not very knowledgeable in the art of high fabric, so this can be forgiven, but then perhaps I should have one of my Dikenian tailors make you something of stronger craft."

But in actuality Erfrant was knowledgeable in the art of high fabric, and he took much hidden offense of Jasper's words. He was quite hurt by them, almost to the point of silent tears, for he was only a child and to be so judged by a fellow child whom he had only just met was unsettling. Now Erfrant was not skilled at crafting friendship, and the observation of the blue carriage was his one chance to initiate camaraderie with Jasper. It clearly failed, and so the two never became friends. Instead, the short walk led Jasper straight to the path of Peril; those two would naturally find common bonds.

"That's Peril of Enceloth," pointed out Erfrant. "His dead father was a dear friend to my father, and so my father thinks that naturally we should share the same bond as they. But he spends all his time shooting at things amidst the trees"—

Jasper was already off. For in Dikenia, all boys were brought up in the skill of forest hunting, and Jasper was no exception. So from this point on the 14 year-old Peril took Jasper into his confidence, finding it easy to sway and play mentor to one nearly half his own age. And Erfrant brushed it off, relieved that he would not have to pretend to be Jasper's friend, and also that Peril now had a hunting partner of his own, so his father might now stop forcing the unwilling friendship upon the both of them.

Now Erfrant may have been tactless in sociality, but he had managed to forge one decent relationship with his distant cousin of the Lycemean branch, Elstone. For while Peril, Jasper, and many of the other children of great lords and nobles hunted and spent long hours out of doors, Erfrant and Elstone both preferred the serenity of four walls. They passed away the hours of bright sun through the filters of cool curtains, and spoke of fabric and cloth, as well diamond and jewel. Already they had strong preference for the colors that would come to define them: blue for Prince Erfrant, and white for lord Elstone.

Undoubtedly the biggest hurdle in the friendship of Erfrant and Elstone was the fact that, unlike Erfrant, Elstone was not a prince. He was the son of a king, yes, but he was born to the house of Lycema. And as Lycema was the great woman-kingdom descended from Naemela, child of Naegeli, it had been law since the nation's founding that always it would be a matriarchy, ruled by daughters of daughters of mothers. And so Elstone felt what it was to be a woman in any other nation, where wermen were the first in line to inherit the throne.

"Woe that I could not have been born to any other nation," he would pout, and Erfrant shrugged it off as the disgruntled miseries of a twelve year-old boy. Surely he would grow out of these feelings of short-handed fate, and would come to be content with his lot as a noble lord of Lycema without any prospects of ruling. Whether or not he did, will be seen by the end of this chapter.

This leads us to Trilsenya, the effortlessly angelic girl of sixteen who would walk through the hall on occasion with simple yet genuine smile, barefoot and freckled, pulling off a slouched demeanor in a way that shunned the norms of high snootery among nobles. All this Prince Erfrant saw and admired, to the disgust of Elstone. "My sister is not beautiful," he would say.

But Erfrant would protest. "If she is not beautiful, then you must say she is sincere, wholesome, authentic, alluring"—

"I will say none of those things. And neither should you, for not only are you a full six years younger, but she's of relation! We're all of relation— you, me, all the nobility of Angelon and Lycema, all descended from Naegeli and Toom."

"That was nine generations ago!" Stammered Erfrant. "Am I to be hammered for seeing true quality in my ninth cousin? Anyway, I've no interest in the things wermen are typically after. You know, like Peril"—

And indeed at that moment Peril of Enceloth was come to make a brash proposal to Tril, for he was at fourteen already fond of women in many ways, but all of them concerning flesh. Trilsenya then did not give much thought to Peril. "Go back to playing with that little white Dikenian boy," she would say. "He's the best you'll get."

After some days in Arthconendin, Wheatlank daughter of Witlonk Firespear arrived. Now fourteen— the same age as Peril— she had been orphaned at the age of five when her brave and heroic father was slain in 2291. Now she was grown into one fierce and already with the chill of battle and wind in her eyes, and she rained red hair all out from her pores, even in places where women might not normally sprout. Therefore she quickly acquired the name Wheatlank the Unshaven, though her few friends such as Princess Trilsenya called her Lanny.

So of the seven children at Arthconendin we have now mentioned, easily they broke into pairs as follows: Erfrant and Elstone, Tril and Lanny, Peril and Jasper. And then there was Himgo, second son of Wilderfrant, all alone muttering made-up words to himself for he was too young to be included in anything.

Now that the stage is mildly set, we will take an eventful page from the memoirs of Jasper, wherein he and Peril were hunting in the woods as was commonplace. What was not commonplace on this day was that Peril spoke aloud his mind to rape the princess Trilsenya. At this, Jasper— being wise beyond his years— pointed out that it would be to no one's advantage to rape the princess.

"Yes, I suppose there are consequences," went Peril, "But in my mind, after she feels firsthand how tender of a touch I have to offer, she will find no fault in it. And then her and I might come to join our kingdoms of Enceloth and Lycema, and then split them apart once more when we have both a son and a daughter to take them. Doesn't it sound glorious?"

And here Jasper is said to have pointed out the many flaws in Peril's thinking. He suggested instead that Peril take a trip to a penetration tavern. "I'm only fourteen," responded Peril. "Don't tell me you've been to a penetration tavern?" And indeed Jasper had, for it was customary in Dikenia for young boys to lose their virginities quite early.

"But you do not clearly see my mind," spoke Peril. "For I have no desire to lie with tavern girls; there is an exclusivity that I seek with the princess Tril. And whereas when you first arrived it was a matter of flesh, I now feel that over the course of these last many weeks I have developed a thirst for her spirit, her soul, and her mind. It is not all that simple to explain. But when I look upon her now, I see far more than I had before."

"This all may be true," nodded Jasper, "but all the same, do not rape her."

And this was all the counsel he was willing to provide, for fear that those four words would become lost if he spoke more, but also because young Jasper truly did not understand what Peril was speaking of. He was a Dikenian, and Dikenians were not for sentimentality in the slightest. As previously stated, they were abundant in penetration taverns and willingly invited their young in to enjoy them. They did not marry, or at least not in the tradition of the nations descended from Angelon. There were rituals of companionship, but the average Dikenian might have upwards of twenty lifetime companions. And these were seen as partners strictly for the purposes making of men, with sentimentality shunned.

So when Peril went on about passion of the spirit and notions of love, Jasper could in none of the ways relate. His heart was made of stone, he joked, and truly he would be impervious to feelings of adoration until the year 2323. At the time, he saw women and wermen alike simply as figures in either the arena of politics or sex, and there was nothing else. For he was of the proud race of Dikenians: swift and independent in their governance, quick and detached in their intercourse. And all the while as he said these things, he bade constant reminder that Peril should not rape Trilsenya.

Peril must have forgotten.

On a cloudy windy day at Arthconendin, the elders held council in the Grand Hall, studying maps and letters, discussing how they might wisely go about battling Haegos and any hopes they might have of besting him. Obviously the room was tense, and this was not an ideal time— nor are any— for a sixteen year-old girl to come crashing through the doors, accusing a fellow prince of molestation. All of those in attendance save one were at a loss for words, many probably under the warped opinion that one rape was nothing on the canvas of atrocity that Haegos was presently committing, being they were all so wrapped up in tales of his mass torment just moments ago. But King Wilderfrant was not so perplexed, and managed to rise within a single moment upon hearing the news, ever able to snap himself into the proper mindset for whatever needed being done.

"Where is he?" Asked Wilderfrant as he marched through the woods. Trilsenya pointed to an upright stone, and there Wilderfrant found a hiding Peril, whom he took up by the nostrils and dragged to the hall of chamber pots. There, he cited the ancient law of his kingdom, laid down by Wilderfrant the First, and since put out of commission. But he declared it would be revived on this day, for Arthconendin was outside the jurisdiction of any kingdom, and Wilderfrant the high king of all present. So he passed sentence and made for an equal retribution. For Peril's crime of molestation, he himself would be raped. And so entered in Wheatlank or Lanny, who had expressed desire for Peril in the past. Thus on that day, two occurrences of unwanted intercourse transpired, and for the rest of their days both Trilsenya and Peril would feel both spoilt and ashamed.

But justice was done, and forgiveness in those days was easy among children. Simply put, their fathers and mothers forced them into forgiveness, for they needed no more interruptions— they were carefully plotting courses of war that would either save or destroy their lands, and the children understood this. They understood that whatever differences they might have, or what offenses might have been committed, all their issues were now quite petty when viewed from the vast stage of the war which now threatened to leave all of Denderrin Othim in flame.

So with the coming of the changing season, where leaves grew orange and brown, and fell off trees leaving deep piles amidst the ground, they all sat together at Arthconendin. They found a great circle of ancient stones, and not knowing what they were for or who had put them there, began to talk and make up stories of the past. They all found the means to laugh. Erfrant forgave Jasper for his pretentiousness, Elstone forgave his sister for her coveted position as heir to Lycema, Peril forgave Lanny for raping him in retribution for his respective rape, and— most miraculous of all— Trilsenya even, on the surface at least, forgave Peril for ravishing her body.

But of course these moments of laughter lasted not long at all. For they were amidst dark times, and their fathers and mothers were grim with sleepless faces. The demeanors of the children soon followed. And they began to discuss what might come to pass should the conflict rage on into their own times of adulthood. How long would each of them last? Would their homelands ever be taken, and if so where then would they go? Would the alliances in place on that day survive the passing of the present kings? Talking over all, the heirs to the kingdoms agreed upon one thing: that they would be ever faithful to one another and all of them sworn enemies to the aims of Haegos. Thus ended their stay in Arthconendin.

Years swept away and the aspirations of the great lords at Arthconendin were shown to be fruitless. They had sworn to all stand together in one great alliance, for it was decided that only in that strength that Haegos might be bested. But Haegos foresaw this, and split his own armies, sending them out wide across the map. The defensive armies were forced to disband and each to their own they went, defending from attack along their own borders. Lycema lost city after city along the sea coast until stood Medwyn alone, Enceloth was besieged from the north, Dikenia felt the constant throttle from its many borders with Mangiloth. And Angelon— largest and strongest of the eastern nations— was under attack primarily to its northwest, for shortly after Arthconendin the forces of Haegos had sailed up the Swifting and sacked the towns of Softwind and Dogrape.

But for all the horrors of Haegos slowly gnawing away at the borders of all his adversaries, there was yet still peace in the quiet capitals of these lands. One could stand in Frawlin, for example, and still watch the slow seasons change to the gentle flow of the Fickling Stream. And this is where King Wilderfrant VII would spent his changing seasons, always returning from war at the end of the breeze and leaving again right before the winds. For no man can spend all the year in battle, without taking enormous toll upon his own strength and spirit. In late 2309, Wilderfrant returned to meet his first grandson— or flopdown, as they called them in Angelon— DANE, the surprisingly early offspring of Himgo the Tall. Seeing as Himgo had already delivered, Wilderfrant paid his eldest son a visit and thought he might try his luck there.

"You lag on your duties, my blue prince," jested Wilderfrant, now just receiving his first silvers in his 54th year. "Already your brother has succeeded in bringing me a flopdown!"

"Do not hold me to that bizarre standard, it is an anomaly by all sense that Himgo should have achieved such deed by the age of thirteen, and I daresay probably only being in that he is very tall."

And so Wilderfrant patted his eldest upon the cheek, knowing well not to expect a child from that boy's loins any time soon. For Erfrant had never shown any physical attractions— not to women, not to wermen, nor anything in between. He simply liked music, and he simply liked fabric. And plays and pageantry, one might well assume. But he did not like the act of making men at all; he found it atrocious.

How was he to continue the family line then? Well, surprisingly to some, the swelling of genitalia need not be harbored exclusively by the sight, thought and touch of delicious folk. For Erfrant, something else entirely would be needed— the things that made his wermanhood swell were birds. Blue-feathered Ekharts, to be precise. And not the similar Blue-feathered Befferts, for these had no potency.

All in the prince's household found the matter equal parts bizarre and disturbing. "You want... to make men with a bird?" Asked one of the elder generation.

"Impossible even if I tried," corrected Erfrant. "But no, I simply become aroused... by these birds. Blue-feathered Ekharts, they are the pinnacle of Athrallia's creation. It is not by any dirty thought that I crave this; I do not contrive to hold them in my hands or put them where they need not be put. I simply go to a higher place when I see them dancing upon leaves. 'Tis the beauty makes me cum."

And so, after repeating what it was that might make him cum — a hundred times or more to various officials— the process was at last put into motion. A team of wilderfolk was assembled to journey up the western ridge of the Angelocs, trying their best not to fall in the battles which raged nearby, until they came to the tropical Eastern Green Woods. There they toiled long in the wet forest, searching for Blue-feathered Ekharts, and once they found, they then had the daunting task of catching some. An entirely separate book could be written upon the difficulties these folk must have faced in retrieving the prince's Blue-feathered Ekharts.

Once the Ekharts arrived in Frawlin, Erfrant readied himself. The entire city stood by, now waiting for him to send forth ejaculation. He sued for privacy. The peoples obeyed. And there in the eery quiet, Prince Erfrant of Angelon cried for he did not believe he could arouse himself enough to provide what his people sought. They were only birds, after all.

What happened next is a matter of debate. Some say Erfrant received a divine vision from Athrallia, and saw the future outwards of forty generations. Some say that he inhaled the potent juices of the Feepberry, and this is what brought on the visions and the cum. Others say that he simply did the deed immediately, without complication. Regardless of how it passed, it did indeed come to pass. And the members of his household swiftly collected Erfrant's fluid, quickly pouring them down into the canals of a harlot deemed most virtuous.

This most virtuous of harlots, then, would come to be the mother of Wilderfrant IX, or the Stone King, as history would remember him. But he does not figure into this chapter.

The logical place to continue the narrative finds its place in the year 2319, with the child lords of Arthconendin all now in the prime of their ages. The war had taken a turn for the worse in the past decade, and even Angelon proper was so overrun at this point that the only free lands in the kingdom now lay within a small circle of last defenses, centered around Frawlin. The Children of Arthconendin wrote often to each other at first, but as the conflict became more desperate even this was hard to achieve. Nonetheless, it was agreed by all that it was time for all their forces to pool together and engage Haegos outright. Eventually all the Children of Arthconendin received word to assemble at Jasper's residence in Dokkum, far out of reach from the enemy.

Erfrant and Elstone made the long journey together, and spoke over fond memories of their youth. At first heavily guarded by legions of riders, as they ventured deeper and deeper into Dikenia they felt enough comfort to lag off from their escorts. By the time they arrived on the tree-planted path outside Dokkum, it was just the two of them. As they crossed a small bridge, they saw a white palace between two trees, with a modest entrance sloping upwards into a very tall backside. They laughed aloud at the peculiar design of the place, and of the color.

"I almost didn't you see you there, Jasper!" Shouted Elstone. "For your skin is so white and your palace is— also white, and the shades are near inseparable, is this of purposeful design?"

"Of route. If Haegos should ever make it this far I can always remain hidden; he'd never see me so long as I stand up against my own home."

"The time for joking is over," stated a solemn Erfrant, after only one joke. "Jasper, it is good to see you. But tell us of your wars with Mangiloth."

"Yes, well you will be pleased to hear it, and I do speak with sincerity. For while you unlucky bastards have seen nothing but defeat on all sides, the land of Dikenia has grown once again strong. We have not been battered so easily, and under my command these peoples have proven time and time again the saying that Dikenia is the golden jewel of warrior nations. Haegos was ill to rouse revolt in his old homeland of Mangiloth — for we Dikenians are of a superior breed and will best the Mangilothians any day!"

"It is refreshing to hear your confidence, Jasper," spoke Erfrant, "But there is more to the world than Dikenia or Mangiloth."

"That I know, but you didn't allow me closure. I have subjugated Mangiloth, taking all their soldiers and making them my own. We now have a doubled army in the far east."

"And why would you count a subjugated army as yours to hold? Standings may shift fast in this long-enduring struggle, especially from those who never held your way to begin with."

"But it is the nature of Dikenians to be completely subservient to their masters," explained Jasper. "And the peoples of Mangiloth have now become Dikenian; proudly will they remold themselves, for we are of the prouder, more dignified peoples."

"Very well," trailed off the voice of Erfrant, as he caught sight of Trilsenya, now a king of Lycema in her own right. To say she had grown more beautiful would be an insult to her past selves in all their incarnations. She had not grown more beautiful— for this was impossible— but she had simply retained beauty, and Erfrant took obvious notice.

"I hear you conceived your son by looking at a pair of birds," smirked Jasper. "Tell me, do you wish it would have been her? Is she the only one you would have settled for? It's all well, we are close friends, you may confide in me."

But Erfrant was not so sure he could. Still Jasper was the same as he was nineteen years ago, frank and of high intelligence, with a noble compass, yet at the same time cold, and mysterious. Perhaps reserved. And above all very proud. This aspect of his personality had grown the most in the years since Arthconendin, aided very clearly in his good chance with his military exploits.

That night, Trilsenya walked along Jasper's garden with her brother Elstone. The two royal siblings of Lycema had been estranged for some years, with Elstone serving King Wilderfrant in Angelon while Trilsenya ruled her own nation from Isha Sa. There were raw feelings between the two, for Elstone had sought to hold some territory in Lycema in his own right, despite tradition stating that women would rule in all instances over the claims of wermen. Elstone openly disputed this, claiming that quality should preside first over gender. To this Trilsenya had replied that Elstone had not yet presented any form of superior quality to the woman nobility already in place.

"Do you repent from what you said those nine years ago?" Asked Elstone as they walked through Jasper's peaceful paths.

"I do not believe 'repent' is the right word. I meant what I said at the time. Perhaps now you have bettered yourself. But how would I be one to know, since for these nine years of my reign you have hid yourself my sight?"

Elstone fumed, but controlled himself. "I have been at war, these past nine years Tril! In the leading ranks of the Young King Wilderfrant the Glorious, and not yet have I fallen! 56 and two thousand Desiroth have I slain, and here I stand. Is that not proof of my valor, sister?"

Trilsenya examined the face of her dramatic younger brother. She felt his warm red cheek with her hand. "You are brave, Elstone. And in battle I'm sure there is no equal. But to rule a kingdom, you must have more skill than that. From the high seats of Lycema we find mastery through strategy, and cunning. I do not belittle you, brother, but know that I and my barons have done a fine job without you all these years and are continuing to do a fine job now."

And so came the departure of Elstone. Out for an extension to his walk, was supposed at the time. But he was not back by morning, and to where he fled none then knew.

Some days later, Peril of Enceloth arrived. And like Erfrant, long passing years had not stilled his love for Trilsenya. Unlike Erfrant, however, Peril was desirous and lustful, and unable to retain his duty in the face of pretty face.

"Lady Trilsenya. What a pleasure it is to see you here," were his words to the gorgeous king.

"Were you expecting not to see me here? After all I am a king now."

"As am I," smoothly spoke Peril. "And perhaps we had better discuss the prospects of uniting our realms of Lycema and Enceloth, to the glory of"—

"We are at war, Peril. An alliance between our kingdoms is implied, as we are both fighting a mutual threat. And if we do not prevail, I'm afraid neither one of us shall ever marry or reproduce."

"You are 35!" squinted Peril, ornery with frustration. "If you do not come to make men on this night, then I do not believe you ever will! For the time has almost certainly passed you by!"

And in this way Peril drove Trilsenya from an uneasy acquaintance to one who would no longer allow him in her sight.

Meanwhile, the Lord of the Longpis arrived, and pledged his full support from across the Gizle. This Longpis Lord was Vilan, son of Hipfinger, who had been made an orphan in his infancy.

"You could say this fight is indeed personal to me then," spoke Vilan. "But also I come because Haegos has wrested from us our lovely town of Lay Pork. He holds it now for his Mountain Men, whom he has recruited to war from the high Sashites. I do believe that Lay Pork would surely be a good place to channel our efforts— not just for the sake of getting a beloved town back on our map, but also because Haegos has put up a new tower there, right on the southern edge of the Deepest Pits. He's got the bulk of his resting army there from what we can tell, and he'd never expect an attack from the south, what with all his foes fighting so far north."

Erfrant, Jasper, and Trilsenya each considered this in their own way. "We would have to strike fast, if we were to truly catch Haegos off his guard," surmised Erfrant.

"How can we trust this Longpis Lord," asked Jasper, doubtful of Vilan's intentions. "He could be conspiring with the enemy and leading us into evil."

"I believe the logic is sound, but we must prepare our forces first," spoke the voice of Trilsenya. "If we are to risk open battle, we must be assured of victory. And if we are to obtain victory, we want it to be one so crippling as to wipe Haegos off his throne forever."

At this moment, Peril leaped in through the window. All were startled and wet.

"There is no time to waste in gathering forces! Erfrant is right, the greatness of this plan lies in the surprise. Let us ride now together to Lay Pork and slay the demon Haegos for once and evermore! If you do not consent, it is no matter to me. I shall take my own forces hence, and Enceloth will rule the day. And then, Trilsenya, you will rue the words that fell from your mouth! You will bitterly regret your denial of me! For I will rise to unrivaled glory as the king who smote Haegos to the ground!"

Peril, in all ways, accomplished none of this.

He did in fact ride swift to the Gizle, and with his whole army behind marched past the captured town of Lay Pork and right up to the gates of the new Tower of Haegos.

"Send out your worst, Haegos Demoncraft! For my men are well fed and rested, and stretch the entire width of your plain. We will march forward regardless of your action, and take this tower for the holy land of Enceloth! Come out from your tower and face us in the flesh! Down with your banners and out with your inners! That is the song we sing."

And Peril smirked a devilish grin as his army behind let out giddy cheers of thunder. The gates of the tower began to open, and Peril made ready for the inevitable moment when Haegos would walk upon the earth, in which he would charge and stab him through with his silver lance.

But that moment never came. Instead of Haegos emerging out of the tower in a state of surrender, it was Melizar. And never did she in all her existence once think of such a thing.

She rode forth on a giant steed, seated upon a many-pronged steel chair, and wearing a terrifying antlered crown. Her eyes pointed downward at all those who stood short below, she stopped before Peril of Enceloth.

"Bow," was all she said.

Trembling, Peril of Enceloth stepped down from his horse, confused, but weak above all else. "Who are you?" He put to Melizar, enthralled in her majesty. But she merely looked away, scanning the army of Enceloth with sharp and apathetic eyes. Peril repeated the question, but under the gaze of Melizar he understood.

"Right, you want for me to bow." And bow he did, kneeling at the feet of Melizar, as she lowered her thick sword to Peril's eyes.

"Now kiss," she spoke, and Peril kissed the steel blade. Melizar shook her head, and out from between her fiery lips dropped a long thin tongue, moving as if it truly were some intoxicating snake. Peril nodded, and then proceeded to lick Melizar's sword. She turned the sword, so that the sharp of the blade now touched Peril's tongue. Still he rode up with the same lick, and his tongue bled out, almost split down the middle by the time he reached the hilt.

"Tell me Peril of Enceloth, did you really think it was Haegos that commanded such forces? Such power that could start in such darkness, and spread into all the corners of your world? You believe that of a crippled mortal, locked inside a black steel covering? Well now you see the truth."

And she lifted Peril onto the back of her steed, placing his hands around her. "Yes, now I see the truth," whispered Peril as he gazed into the infinite pools of Melizar's eyes.

"Come then. Now you are home. You will serve me truly?"

"All the days of my life."

Melizar smiled. She was pleased that her spells of enchantment were once again—

"If," put in Peril, "I can see what lies under there." And his finger drifted downwards on Melizar.

The Primordial Starling was swiftly broken out of her contentment, and now spoke plainly. "Yes. Of course you will.

You can take whatever you want, live in my tower forever if you'd like. On the simple condition that you order your army now to disband."

And so Peril descended and walked back to his commanders. "Turn back, for I delve into this tower now alone. You cannot come with me, nor would I wish it upon you." And he feigned a sob. And then abruptly quit and marched away.

"Yes, his strategy is to murder the evil queen in her own bed!" surmised the smiling first commander.

But Himgo the Tall, second commander to Peril and brother to Prince Erfrant, shook his head. "Have you not long known this king? Peril is a man of the flesh and if it looks as though he has just abandoned his cause for the sake of holy cunt, then there is no other motive. He has simply done just that."

And so was the army of Enceloth finished off without fight.

The news of Peril's voluntary capture spread fast through all the lands, for Melizar made it so. She found it gleeful to expose the disgraced king for the wretch he was, and forged letters of all kinds to send to the seven winds.

"This whole affair is preposterous," spoke Erfrant with the slamming of a fist. Trilsenya concurred. And Jasper, proud as he was, thought it was his place to rescue his old friend from the confines of that storied tower.

"No Jasper," warned Erfrant. "Already we have one king taken captive on account of Melizar's beauty."

"Blame not the beauty of Melizar, but the lust of men," replied Jasper.

"But still, let us not risk another. Not until we have gathered all our forces. It is clear by these letters that Melizar and Haegos mean to lure us down to Lay Pork, surely for a night of evil business."

"Ho!" Laughed Jasper. "Evil business? Evil business is upon us at every hour! It is happening now as we speak and closing in on our capitals like a rope around a hardened flip. Reports from Enceloth say there was no army in sight of that tower— if I ride down with all the men of Dikenia, we will put a swift end to the makers of this war and thus regain peace. Do not worry yourselves on my resolve. My heart is of stone, remember? I am not taken by women, neither by their beauty or their words. They hold no sway over my vast pride and objective."

"This is true," observed Trilsenya. "Jasper has proven himself resilient to all forms of courtship."

Jasper nodded with a smile. "No tower wench will halt me at the gates."

And so Jasper repeated the course of Peril, albeit with an army three times the size. All the loyal men of Dikenia rode behind the proud tall man with the pale white skin and the pure black hair flowing in the sunlight, long enough to reach down to his ass, which he took to calling the Crack of Doom.

Upon the wide expanse of flat plain lay the Tower of Haegos, and Jasper led the way across the field of black pebbles. His armor was valiant, with thick plates of silver and gold. And as his horse trotted leisurely up to the tower, he knew he had the full support of all the lines behind him. In this way he stopped before the quiet tower, and projected upwards, just as Peril had done:

"You have something of mine. An old friend. Peril? Can you hear me?! I've heard tell that this vile man has locked you in her chamber, and is tormenting you day and night. Tell her now to reveal herself, to step forward and speak true. For we shall storm the tower if our demands are ill met. We are men of Dikenia! And our fire shall consume all that stands before!"

And so, in the same fashion as with Peril, Melizar rode out in grand fashion. This time, she wore even more exquisite robes, revealing in parts the even more exquisite vision of her tantalizing skins.

But Jasper only smirked. "You are full of cock indeed if you think you can ride out and plummet me from my principles so easily," coldly spoke Jasper. "After all, what are you? Finely dressed man on a large horse? I would argue my armor shines brighter than your robes. And my horse is assuredly faster. Why don't you come bow to me, Melizar?"

It irked the Starling to see one so full of pride, and unwilling to immediately unhorse and bow before her."So you wish to do battle then? Surely there is no other way to settle this."

And Melizar put a trembling hand down onto her sacred of sacreds, and revealed just enough so that Jasper alone saw everything.

But true to his word, Jasper was unswayed.

"Surely there isn't," he shrugged. And then a charge commenced. All the forces of Dikenia rode like skyfire onto the single tower, hacking down the singular man where she stood. The tower was under swift siege which lasted only minutes, for the strength of Dikenia was overwhelming. And when all was secure, Jasper searched every chamber for his dear friend Peril. But here Peril was not.

Discouraged but not put out, Jasper navigated his forces up the western side of the Deepest Pits, seeking out the citadel of Crissen, and hoping to find better fortune there. Indeed, upon arrival at Crissen, he saw vast camps of Desiroth and Vexen sprawled about. Jasper charged his legions forth and then halted them when all of the enemy was held in a chokehold.

"Each of you will provide testimony today!" Screamed Jasper, red with fierce anger. "You will tell me where my friend and brother is! Hand over Peril of Enceloth, and all other captives you hold! Then you will divulge all your knowledge— all of you — on where your armies lie!"

And the Vexen commander, with swords upon his neck, released the only three captives he swore to be in holding there. Out came two naked girls, aged merely twenty, and badly bruised with dirt thrown all up upon. Jasper, occupied with other doings, glanced up and saw them. Pitiful, he thought to himself, and maybe a little sad. But those were the extent of his thoughts.

Until the third girl rose up, up from the ground. Jasper caught the full motion, and as he watched her rise up from the ground he felt a strange twinge upon him. It was the loosening of his agony, for he had long kept any and all feelings of sadness locked deep within him, revealing himself in only pride and strength. But looking into the eyes of this abused, scared and helpless girl, he shed tear.

Jasper invited the girl to his tent. There, she was bathed, and fed, and attended to with great care. Jasper did not enter until his presence was requested, and there he was shocked to see the girl completely well, making small splashes in the water as she feasted upon grabes and butter.

"It was a swift recovery then?" Asked Jasper.

"For who? Me? I never really had it that bad," she shrugged, talking quickly and off the whim, as young girls often do. "Would you like to touch my breasts?" And she plopped up, making a great splash of water, pulling Jasper forward and wetting his entire face. He laughed in sheer shock, but then looked up into the eyes of the young girl. He could tell this was a genuine sense of playfulness, and took the queue to play along.

In this way, the young girl pulled Jasper into the basin with her and lowered his guard, laughing at first to the tune of the dumbest of things. Jasper was relieved to be with someone so light and gentle and innocent of the world, for he had spent all his long years in solitude and utter misery, being solemn even when he was a child and ought to have been enjoying his time. Slowly though, did the countenance of the girl change from joy and rascality to a more thoughtful, philosophical light. And here, Jasper was amazed to see that not only did he find this girl alluring, but also did he agree with her in all ways. Everything she said— every allegory, every theory, every observation she put upon the world— it all struck a perfect chord with the Dikenian king.

The night passed on quick, and the two remained in warm water through the fifth, sixth, and even seventh hour. But it was then, when the moon was shining at its fullest, that the voice of the young girl began to change. And as drifting cloud happened then to cover dimming stars, Jasper thought he saw a change of face. In the growing darkness he strained his eyes.

"What's the matter?" Asked the girl. "Can't you see?"

"I— no, I can see. I'm, just, having a little trouble— comprehending, I mean to say I'm confused." And as his focus returned, the body he lay upon looked as one he had seen before. He shook his head, pressed his eyes, and sat up upon the ledge.

"The water isn't too hot now, is it?" Asked the woman. "You found it so nice and soothing before." And with long soft fingers she clasped the back of Jasper's neck, fingers so compelling that he was brought down fully upon her. He felt then the pull of something sweet beyond words, under the scented water, and as he exhumed his deep and buried pleasure, he released all into the cradle of this powerful life force. When Jasper reopened his eyes, he saw that it was Melizar in the basin.

Unwillingly his lips began to quiver, and he sobbed unendingly, letting off all the pain that had stuck to him for 28 years of earthly existence. Melizar put gentle hands on him and brought his head down upon her chest, a mother now of great comfort. "You are forgiven," she whispered serenely in his ear. But still Jasper sobbed, until the untainted voice of his first and only love carried him to netherworlds of rest and calm, and perfect peace.

On the Battle of Lay Pork

And now we come to it. The thunder of that generation, which sounded out in horror so loud that the reverberations have cast themselves down into even our own time. Yet those who have not heard the tale will laugh. To hear of a place and a battle with a name so infantile.

Indeed, when children learn their histories they will often exclaim in unison, "Speak now to that famous battle of old, Lay Pork!" to which any reasonable teacher will reply, "I'm afraid the story of that dreaded night would make your eyes bleed with sorrow." But still the children long to hear it, and indeed once it is told, all in attendance feel gut-spun and the heartbound spend the greater part of six minutes in solid lamentation.

Perhaps those who rode south from Angelon in those days made the same naive assumption— that the Battle of Lay Pork was destined to be a great and triumphant victory, for how could such a name breed anything less than a playful-hearted outcome?

Three years had passed since Jasper's campaign to the Tower of Haegos. As painted in the previous chapter, he was seduced by Melizar, in a basin, and that proved to be no mere single-night seduction. It continued until days turned to weeks and months to seasons, until Jasper was in the full service of the dark sorceress. This turning was in all ways different then the capture of Peril, whom was kept still in Melizar's presence as well.

For where Peril had been commanded to break apart his army immediately and indefinitely— a thing which he rightforth agreed to— Jasper had been told to retain his position as leader of the Grand Dikenian Army. For the Dikenians held absolute loyalty to their king, and Melizar knew as long as Jasper remained under her control, so too did that sweeping expanse of pale-skinned warriors.

Also contrasting from the situation of Peril, Jasper was not held in a cage. He was free to roam at will, and conduct business with the neighboring kingdoms of the realm, for Melizar placed in him full trust. She respected Jasper, and some would even go on to observe that this respect might even be counted as love, if indeed Melizar was capable of such a thing. If ever a werman she did spill out sentiment for, however, Jasper was he.

Because of Jasper's continued presence in the war councils of Angelon, Lycema and the Longpis, men like Prince Erfrant had no reason to doubt his continued loyalty to the fight against Haegos. When questioned on the details of his assault on the Tower, Jasper always maintained that a blockade had been established before the tower, and that they must wait for Lay Pork to be emptied before another assault was to be tried. King Wilderfrant and Erfrant had no reason to doubt this testimony, for the entirety of his army swore it to be so as well.

The year was 2323, then, when Jasper informed the stunted nation of Angelon that the time to strike had come. A mighty army was assembled, and the old King Wilderfrant VII— ironically still calling himself the Young King— rode south along with his son Erfrant and King Trilsenya of Lycema. Instead of rounding the tip of Cathuma at Medwyn and traveling south directly to Lay Pork, they were compelled to take the long road along the sea. For the eastern beaches of Nephinarthos were held in a choke of submission by the fattest of the tyrant's army.

The road around the sea was not much better. None of the towns on the coast save Medwyn were then free of Haegos' forces, and the Angelon armies would travel only little by little in darkness, spending the days in slumber under what shelters they could find. They had tried to disband their forces in daylight so as to hide their true numbers, but too often did skirmishes then erupt with the Vexen and Desiroth warlords, and too often were good soldiers needlessly picked off and eaten for no good cause. So then as the army rounded out the southern edge of the sea and walked along the foothills of the eastern Sashites, they stayed all together.

"So much for our idea of surprise," muttered Erfrant on a cold night spent sleeping against jagged black stone, as rain poured from the open sky. This was anything but the kind of night he was used to, having grown up in splendor even for a prince, and much preferring his furdle and sloot to the roads of wrath.

"It cannot be helped," spoke his father the king. "By now they have certainly sent word to Haegos of an approaching army, but they do not necessarily know that once we arrive, our forces will be more than tripled, as we are joined by the men of the Longpis and Jasper's marvel of Dikenia."

"How do we know that Jasper will not let us down?" Asked Erfrant. "It will take skillful timing, or else we may be cut off upon the Gizle before we even make it to Lay Pork."

"The road will be open, my young prince. For Jasper has created a diversion north of the Deepest Pits, and drawn them out towards the Rounds. As long as we keep our steps swift we will arrive just as he intended, and the fields before the Tower of Haegos will be open to us."

The speed of the Angelon army excelled as they reached the great River Gizle, and on their third night traversing its course, the company beheld the most glorious of sunsets. The sky bore clouds all across except for the very bottom of their view, where a blazing purity of orange struck them as a divine sight, akin perhaps to the fabled urine of the Twelve Lords. Rising from this orange purity were soft orange brushes against the clouds, as if Lyvierfania the sky goddess were stroking them gently with her finger. And above this, the orange gave way to pink, and the clouds became more like long stretches of cotton, growing rougher above their heads yet inviting all the same.

This was the last sunset viewed by many of them, and one that Erfrant had wished he could have captured. "If only there were a way to gaze upon a perfect evening air, and preserve the image so that all those down along the line of time could see for themselves," he lamented, and then ordered that any man among them who could wield a paintbrush do so in an effort to replicate the sight. But even as an entire host of burly warriors lifted their paints, already was the sky changed. Such is the nature of this world, that the finest of moments last only long enough for one to decide they ought to try and catch it. But by the time any net is raised, the moment is already far hidden away in the thick trees, never to be captured.

The next day— the Ninth of Lurvarion— Wilderfrant, Erfrant, Trilsenya, Vilan of the Longpis and Jasper of Dikenia led the way up a hill of wooded rock on the north shore of the Gizle. Over a crest and down across a great flat plain lay the Tower of Haegos, nestled between small black peaks which led into the Deepest Pits. Off to the side, sandy cliffs and caverns held the captured town of Lay Pork just out of view. As the moon did its setting and the sun began to rise, the armies of Angelon aligned in their ranks.

Jasper was placed at the very point of all the forces, his Dikenian expansing sprawling out behind him like wings, forming the entirety of the front lines. Stationed behind them in the center were the forces of Angelon. And the left and right branch were comprised of the Lycemeans, one branch captained by King Trilsenya and the other by her trusted ally and friend of long years, Wheatlank the Unshaven. The soldiers of the Longpis were held back along the shores of the Gizle, to be used as relief should their comrades become overwhelmed. But such an outcome was not upon anyone's mind, for the full breadth of the assembly stretched all along the back hills bordering the Gizle, and when all at once charged the Tower it would surely be overrun.

The sun shone dim even as the hour of midday approached, and here at last emerged ambassadors of Haegos, willing to speak. What came as a complete shock to Erfrant was that, among these vile creatures, was none other than his old friend from youth, Elstone of Lycema. The jealous brother of Trilsenya had found refuge in the camp of Haegos, and here had been promised real power, and the power to overthrow his sister and wrest from her the kingdom of Lycema that he might then rule under his own line.

He approached slowly, Elstone, with a face of snobbery. His silky pure white robes reflected all what light came to that valley, and contrasted enormously with all the black around. It was miraculous that it had not then grown dirty.

"Still wearing blue," he smirked to Prince Erfrant, "the same blue of four-year-old children, and in the same simplistic light. It may have suited you fine in Frawlin but you are sorely misplaced in this dark and dusty land."

"Not so misplaced as you," spoke Erfrant. "You're a fool to think your adoration of spotless white could it ever mix well in a place such as this."

For well over an hour did these exchanges build, with Erfrant and Elstone battling not with swords but with their wits, and all the time Trilsenya looked away, angry and distraught that her little brother had so willingly betrayed her. Jasper tried to comfort her.

"Yes, it is all in vain, those words that were spoken years ago at Arthconendin. Those children who spoke of everlasting brotherhood are not the same. But though Peril and Elstone have been swayed to the side of our enemy, we will rule the day. They are only stalling." And he smiled in his heart, for none yet suspected him of his own treachery.

Meanwhile, the sky grew once again dark. Thick grey clouds strung a carpet above them, giving no hint to the existence of any sun. And Erfrant marched back to his curious and impatient father, who had begun shaking upon his horse, beginning to dread the day and feeling as if he had seen perhaps one too many battle in his time. "What is it, son? A surrender?"

"Hardly, but there'll be no fight today. Not for you anyway. Not for any of you!"

And all the men were confused. Prince Erfrant clarified, that the two princes had come to an agreement. They were to battle one another, in a ring of truth, and the kingdom of the fallen prince would then be forfeit. This was spoken for the benefit of all, that there would be no loss of life on either side save whichever prince fell to the other. But to this Wilderfrant wept. "I would not so soon risk the life of my heir!"

"But it would be risken anyway, Father. It is a risk just to be here upon this field! And how many of these other lives would you then be casting away? Let me put my life upon the bet, and I will best this traitor."

"And if you should lose?"

"Even should I fall, we will lose no more than what is to be lost to us in due time. A kingdom? What good is it to us if they are no men to govern. If I battle Elstone in sole combat, we have the word of Haegos that he will spare all of our people. He will take what lands were ours and we will simply pass into the west, where we might live in peace"—

"As Mountain Men?!" Objected King Wilderfrant. "The word of Haegos?! His word is death, now until his own! We cannot trust that promise. And I will not sacrifice this kingdom! The prophecy of the Mane— be it either trusted or cast out— tells that this great nation will last at least another 51 years. And even then I intend my line to break that prophecy. We cannot simply grant away what is not ours to grant away"—

"Then you are granting away lives! But speak not to me. You are not the true commander of this force. That distinction goes to Jasper of Dikenia, whose army comprises over half of all the men upon this battlefield!" And so Wilderfrant took word with Jasper, who convinced the ailing father to allow the duel.

Erfrant and Elstone stepped into the ring of truth towards the evening, though it seemed already the dead of night. For the sky had grown so dark that no longer did the clouds allow the light of the suns through in any capacity. Flames and torches were then lit all around, and held by the gruesome Desiroth who formed the perimeter, wailing and cheering dreadful cries. Directly behind their vile perimeter was a perimeter of Angelon spearsmen, with their spears pointed directly into the backs of the Desiroth should their vow of peace be broken.

Two great chairs were elevated directly across from one another, over the ring where the two princes were to clash to one's end. On the first chair rose a trembling Wilderfrant, grown nearly as pale as a Dikenian with sickness. He was now truly showing his elderly age, and in every way regretted his coming down to partake in this chapter of the war. Across from him, in the far chair, sat Haegos himself, encased in thick suit of metal overlaid with red cloth and an intricate design of golden twirls.

The blue prince entered into the ring, surely scared. For this was to be the first instance of combat in his life, and this was no mere match. The fate of many kingdoms rested upon his skill with the long silver sword he felt in his shaking hands. The white prince entered in with greater strides of confidence, and an intimidating look with his eyebrows bent down low. Far too low. Erfrant almost laughed to see how hard Elstone was trying in his attempt to look truly sinister. Yet his sword was sinister; there was no mistaking that. A sharpened brown cleaver with 24 jagged blades protruding from each side of the main blade, this was something that Erfrant did not wish to be pierced by—

But he was, almost immediately. Elstone swung the sword and multiple hunks of Erfrant's left arm were ripped off, near the shoulder. Erfrant laughed in pleasant charm, but that is a flourish on my part, for in actuality he shrieked in a bellow of strain. Now this next bit is something that has astounded chroniclers for ages: upon lifting his sword for a second a presumably life-ending hit, Elstone came down fiercely upon the body of Erfrant which had cast to the ground— but the sword was stopped. By Erfrant's own sword.

How Erfrant the sloot-playing blue prince of Angelon managed to block Elstone's blow after having large chunks of arm flesh ripped apart only moments before, no one can clearly say. To speak more to the puzzling nature of it all, this was a young man who had nearly no muscles to speak of. But the gods must have been truly in his blood upon that night, for blue prince Erfrant stood and began to swing his own sword at his distant cousin, grunting ferociously with every blow.

Now did Elstone's pretty white dress finally begin to get dirty. Now did the two princes dance amidst the ring, with their fine fabrics whisping this way and that, as they twirled round and round with the clash of metal. It was quite beautiful, to the eyes of all who could see it. And all the time it was abundantly apparent that this duel was set to the steps of two princes of the arts, who had both spent the majority of their days engaged in the theatre.

But this, being the theatre of war and not of Horlin Deep, did not come to a satisfying conclusion of pomp and splendor. Erfrant finally managed to trip Elstone, and this spelled out his doom. For the white prince Elstone fell straight upon his back. He quickly twisted upwards, but Erfrant was already mid-blow. Elstone raised his sword and stopped a blow to the neck by a single moment, but inches away did Erfrant's sword rest. Erfrant then pushed down upon Elstone, who could not gain proper footing in the pebbly ground. Soon, Elstone's neck was feeling the burn of his sword pushed against it, pushed by the lowering sword of Erfrant.

Friction was building. At last they were there at a standstill, and the next move would prove to be the decisive blow. Then swiftly did Erfrant realize and spin round, avoiding Elstone's blade as it rose up, and then whacking the neck of the white prince upon the return. Elstone fell to the ground this time face first, and did not move but in convulsions, with thick dark blood streaming from his neck.

Most chroniclers choose to omit the following deeds of Erfrant, for his foe being vanquished there really is no true need to include them. But they did occur, as witnessed by the many watching intently around the circle. The blue prince broke into another rage of fury, now screaming outright, and battering his blade down upon Elstone like a hammer, repeatedly cutting into the body of the traitor. The white robes were torn completely to shreds by Erfrant, and the face of the prince disposed of entirely. Only then did Erfrant drop his sword, and look up into the eyes of Haegos.

"Your kingdom is forfeit," is all he said.

Applause erupted from all in the Angelon host, and Wilderfrant let fall joyful drops as he descended from his chair, embracing his son. But swift was Jasper to break the embrace.

"You are a fool if you think this is over!" Warned Jasper.

"But Haegos has retreated back into his towers and we are being showered with jewels and crowns from the enemy," replied Wilderfrant. "My boy has won the fight! Let us now go home!"

But Jasper with serious eyes shook his head. "If you return home on this night, then once again will Haegos rise and plunder your lands. He is not finished, nor will he ever be. We have a force of thousands here on this night; let us end it now for all of time."

And so Jasper convinced Wilderfrant to realign his forces and charge upon the Tower of Haegos after all. Erfrant objected loudly, weeping, crying that all his sacrifice amounted to nothing if the charge took place, and that he would have killed his once-friend in vain. But the words of Jasper sounded the more reasonable— that Haegos had to be destroyed— and so the charge took place.

The numbers that raced forth on the Tower were unimaginable. And if it were not for the treachery of Jasper, surely they would have captured Haegos and razed his havens all upon that single night. The pomp was certainly present. For up upon a great stone, stood the Royal Orchestra of Frawlin, brought with by the insistence of Prince Erfrant. Never before had a grand orchestra accompanied an army into battle, argued Erfrant, and this is what would lead them into triumphant victory.

So the glorious music sounded out across the plains, heralding in the grand charge. But as the magnificent armies rushed forward, to the sound of polished grandeur, Jasper— being the sole leader of the Dikenian ranks— bellowed out a harsh command. Suddenly, all the Dikenians behind veered and started back from whence they came. This was done so swiftly and unexpectedly that there was a massive crash in the middle of the host, where Angelons burst upon the Dikenians who were suddenly riding hard against the current.

The Angelons were surely confused. Those near the back were confused as to the sudden screams and slowing of the rush; those near the front were confused as to why the Dikenians had turned back and started slaughtering them instead of the Haegosians. Wilderfrant, being real damn old, was an insufficient commander and thus the mess only worsened for several minutes, until Trilsenya— far over in the left branch of Lycemeans— got word across to the Angelons.

"You are being slaughtered, turn back! The Dikenians have betrayed you!"

And so the Angelons were sent into a hasty retreat back to the slopes which led to the Gizle. But out of these slopes rambled out strings of Desiroth, this being just as unexpected as the Dikenian betrayal. The Angelons then were trapped in a closing circle of doom, and it was up to the two ranks of Lycema to relieve them. They rushed down hillside and clashed with the lightly-armored Desiroth, smiting many of them to the ground, but the Dikenians they were helpless against.

At this point, the Royal Orchestra of Frawlin was obliterated. For the great rock that they stood upon broke open, cracking into thousands of pieces. Surely this faulty rock was part of the enemy's designs. For while the fortunate were cast down to the ground in a quick death, others fell and were smashed beneath falling boulder, and the more miserable of the lot were swallowed between the cracks of the great stone, to be trapped in narrow crevice as rock slowly wedged upon them and cut into their skins.

It was precisely then that the noble forces of the Longpis rose up on the slopes overlooking the battlefield, and decided to go home. For the night was dark and dreary. A prolonged rain had now begun to fall, and the torches— which provided only the dimmest of lights— were now being put out. Vilan, who had proved himself to be a true Noble Lord of the Longpis Realm and stood beside Prince Erfrant from the beginning, was appalled to glimpse the desertion of his forces as the last of the lights went out. He cursed them all, screaming at the slopes that they would all be made tongueless when their lord returned.

But by this time it appeared that the lords would not be returning home. For the night was now black, not just dark— a starless black when all perception was filled with terrifying shrieks and horrific sounds, and men grew mad not knowing from which direction death would fling out its arms and carry them away to be gnawed upon by sharp teeth. Indeed this was the fear of all upon that night, for the Desiroth— though lightly clad and easily disposable— were stealthy in the dark and would sneak upon their prey without the slightest warning.

This is why the true horrors of the night began when the shrieks were stopped. And all in the dark then was silent. Soldiers told others to hush, needing clarity of the ears to sense when an enemy was near. Then a single howl would cut into the night, of one being dragged away to doom. For the Desiroth were playing a game as it were, and enjoying it immensely, for never before or since had they an entire battlefield of blind men so helplessly waiting to be picked off. One by one did they fall.

And while this heinous snatching of men occurred in the middle of the field, those on the outskirts felt their way around, seeking an escape. Prince Erfrant clutched on tightly to Vilan Lord of the Longpis, and they groped around blindly in the dark. They tried to hold pleasant conversation, but this was difficult considering the circumstances. They then fell into a cave, and here they were fingered by tall creatures of the pits.

Vein-ripper, was the name bestowed upon the crafted demon who lorded over this particular pit and many others. He was made by wicked design by the cunning of Melizar, who sought to raise a swift and fearful creature crafted of pure terror to inflict upon the Angelons. His name in the Sheelkonti Tongue was Branthirin, which translates roughly into the Arc Tongue as "Double Cunt Jim." For this creature of evil design had no eyes, nor mouth nor ears— the sole features on his long wet face were two oval openings, with deep spotted suctions and flaps lining these facial cunts. But his preferred method of execution was not to use his hideous openings, but rather his long and precise fingers, which would slice into the wrist, where the vein would then be suctioned, and ripped out whole.

In this way, Branthirin removed the veins of hundreds, pulling them— often times slowly— clean out of the body through the wrists.

This, then, was a horrifying trial for Vilan and Erfrant. But sadly for the reader and happily for myself, there are no living testimonies of what transpired in that cave, and so I do not feel obliged to relate it.

Leaping over the unknowable, Vilan and Erfrant emerge out of the complex passage of caves after hours of toiling in misery, where they come upon a Lycemean soldier, also escaped from battle.

"Where do you come from?!" Shouted the vomiting Vilan, green with the horror and sickness that comes along with a stroll through the Deepest Pits.

"From the Battle of Lay Pork!" Exclaimed the escaped soldier.

"Of mikkin course you did, darby cosh!" Yelled Vilan, quite profanely. "But do you mean to tell me there's another way around?! Without going through the Deepest Pits?!"

"I suppose I was lucky that way!" Yelled the soldier back. "But we are not clear yet, for now we must follow this ravine, which leads a winding path through the Pits and lets out at the Wheat Fields. Step not in the water, for it is not water— rather a toxic bite that'll burn you straight through."

For many whiles then, Vilan and Erfrant travelled with this boy soldier, and it is from his surviving account that we know of Vilan and Erfrant's tangle in the Deepest Pits with Branthirin. To this boy they also spoke of a bad end they met, which they were also able to escape though they did not say how. One of their paths had led directly into a cave of which there was no way out save the narrow opening they had come through.

There, the hair of the deceased was being piled into the mouths of the taken. Vilan and Erfrant had felt around, only to feel that the prisoners had been stripped, and their bodies now felt of mold and crumbling cracks, with holes and growths, and moist throbbing cyst.

"The hair of the dead was then piled into our own mouths," spoke Vilan, his throat swelling and gagging upon the recollection. "Have you never had one single hair in your food, boy? If it is an especially long hair, and it is not your own, then the sensation is incredibly unpleasant, as you pull it through your teeth and along your tongue to remove from your mouth. Imagine, then, a massive clump of it. Grey and thick, pulled from corpses. And shoved down your throat."

Erfrant puked down the ravine. Then pulled out many such hairs from his mouth, which had been brought up by the vomit.

Had they continued this course with the Lycemean soldier, the pair of them may have lived to old age, and we may have come to know how they miraculously survived the trials they faced in cavern and in pit. But it was not to be, for along a high ridge, Vilan spotted something. It was a Pendalese Maroon, in the full and famous armor for which they are known, and Vilan immediately took it for Shiron.

"That cosh killed my father. My father Hipfinger the First was killed by that!" And he pointed a trembling finger up at the Maroon. He would not be swayed, and so he led Erfrant with him up the ridge, to do battle with this Pendalese Maroon in the starlight. Right did Vilan fight, with the fury of one whose father was slain by whom he presumed to be fighting. And with the Star of Athrallia shining bright above, Vilan pulled away the sword of the Maroon, held his hands, and then thrust his own sword into the helmet, where they eyes of a man would be.

This did nothing. For the armor of the Pendalese Maroons was famed for being impossibly thick, and so it was ridiculous for Vilan to even try. He did, however, succeed in throwing this Maroon to the side, off the ridge, but the Maroon grasped tightly onto Vilan's hand. That then was the predicament, that Vilan had cast his enemy down but in doing so, was to be cast down himself. So reluctantly, Vilan began to cut off his own hand.

"One fell slice!" Advised Erfrant from behind rocks. "He will pull you down the ravine if you take your time with it!"

And this was true, for as Vilan struggled to sever his hand from his wrist, the Maroon grabbed the sword from him and slit the blade right through the narrow opening of Vilan's helmet. His eyes were impaled, and so with a cry and a tumble ended the days of Noble Lord of the Longpis Realm Vilan I, son of Hipfinger, who had also met his end at the hands of a Maroon.

As the sun at last began to rise on that evil night, Prince Erfrant's eyes tracked a group of six horses that raced along the ravine below. He yelled out to them, demanded that they turn back and provide him aid, for he was their prince and now most likely their king, as the fate of his father lie in doubt. Gladly then did the soldiers on horses retrieve the prince, and singing a lament for the thousands of dead they led on. They soon found their path to be blocked by Vexen, and so they turned back, foolish as it might sound, back towards the town of Lay Pork.

The town was charred and broken, with skeletal remains hewing to the buildings of crumbling wood. Prince Erfrant advised that they carry on swiftly, and that a deserted town so near to a site of such viscerally recent devastation was nowhere to linger. Yet the horsemen found it to be a provocative sight, and so they linger they did. They found a cellar full of old monks, with eyes and tongue and nose cut out, and it is on account of these monks that we know of the horsemen's tale.

For too long did they linger in the crumbling streets of Lay Pork; long enough for a heinous roar to be heard on the winds. The Archangel of Cathuma had come.

Chased to the sandy hills above Lay Pork were the horsemen who had rescued Prince Erfrant, and there the Archangel clashed swords with each one of them, before revealing his true form, which may now at last be disclosed. Once he had tired of swordplay, the Archangel dropped his sword, and then did away with the gloves on his hands. Then he would lunge his robed arm forward, the head of his victim would be brought into the sleeve, and there would then be heard a long razing of sharp metal teeth. The head of the victim would then flop out from the Archangel's grasp, the head completely shaved of skin.

The truth of this horror is that large crosses between snake, worm, and eel lie inside the sleeves of the Archangel, with spinning razors of teeth lining the mouths. These were the hands of the Archangel of Cathuma: not hands at all, but rather the smaller two of three heads. For the "head" of the Archangel was not human at all, but just a larger rendition of the snake-worm-eel that commanded the others from a central position.

Upon seeing the faces of his current companions devoured by the Archangel's eel hands, Erfrant once again hid. But the cave in which he took shelter was shallow, and the Archangel approached slowly, knowing well the smell of the prince.

"Already the line is failing," gurgled the three-headed foe. "Where is the courage of the father? Who so nobly won the day at the Wheat Fields? You have proved the old saying. A bad father will produce a noble boy, but a good father, will be doomed to stain the earth with a cowardice offspring."

And in this taunting moments, Erfrant saw a distant glorious future. One where he ruled over a harmonious land, and all swords were laid down and their metal harvested for the building of temples. He haw himself grown old and wise, and telling his flopdowns of the day he lifted up arms against the dreaded Archangel of Cathuma. And these images were enough to inspire the young prince to action. And so he sprung forth out from behind his pillar of salt, up and out of the cave, grasping his sword with a vicious resolve.

But a quick glance at the annals of history will remind us that there is no Wilderfrant VIII. For as the young prince made his decisive leap to action— which in the moment must have felt as if a defining moment of chivalric heroism that would shine as the opening beacon of his reign— he was immediately slain by the Archangel. For as he charged out of his hiding spot, Erfrant was flashed with a gust of dust, the kind which the

Archangel regurgitated especially for princes. And there Erfrant was frozen, his body incapable of movement, covered in this debilitating grey ash.

From here, fire was set to the devastation of Lay Pork, and all in its midst burned. Throughout this, the blue prince stood motionless, unable to close his eyes, seeing all the sadness of the men burning below. The fire climbed the slopes, and soon he too was consumed, though a daring lass carried him to the safety of a tall peak. There, the charred prince, with all his skin gone black and red, breathed his last, and spoke to the lass of his fight with the Archangel, and his vision for future days.

Long was the torment that followed Lay Pork. The free nations of Denderrin Othim were beaten into their capitals, and there they remained as prisoners. For the peoples of Angelon, this meant that their once wide, expansive dominion now consisted of Frawlin, and nothing else. Radiating out from all sides of their last defenses were Vexen encampments, and Haegos roamed freely, inflicting torture upon any found outside that perimeter. In every way it was a hard time, even those who had found refuge in the walls of Frawlin. For in those days the whole of a kingdom was sewn up in that town, and homes which once housed ten now housed a hundred. The streets were full, and food was scarce.

This continued for nine years, until arrived 2232, and the vanishing of King Wilderfrant's patience. His health had declined massively in the wake of Lay Pork, but he was brought to safety by his men on that day. He was grieved to learn of his son's evil fate, and so withered away in his garden. But now in 2232, at the age of 76, he had one final elevation. His youthful spirit revived, he rode out from the crowded waste of Frawlin and journeyed east. The desolation of those lands fueled his anger towards Haegos, and made him conscious that this was to be the last great fight of his life. In a way, the battle against Haegos had consumed all of his days, from his very youth, and he saw no better way to close out his reign than by challenging the demon lord to combat upon his own soil.

Not far into his ride, Wilderfrant was captured, but upon his request he was brought to Ansila Siroth, haven of Haegos in the thin spiraling tower. There, Wilderfrant clashed swords with Haegos in a large cage, quite skillfully for his age. If he had faced down the speechless enemy in younger years, he might have prevailed. But as it were, he was thrown to the floor by the brute of Haegos.

There, Wilderfrant made a final effort to pull from his sack the device he had carried far— the Crown of Ithyendor, which not rested upon the head of a king since the days of the vile Marc Vicar. But if there was a time to use such a desperate weapon, then this was it, as Haegos approached, raising his boot to crush the neck of the elderly king. Wilderfrant smirked aloud, rolling over and lifting the Crown of Ithyendor from its sack, the sudden light blinding all around and sending Haegos aback. But as he placed the crown upon his head, the sheer power of the ancient instrument overcame the body of Wilderfrant. He fainted, falling flat upon his face, and Haegos took the crown for his own.

It was then, when all chance of Wilderfrant's prevailing was extinguished, that Haegos ordered an adjacent wall to be thrashed aside. There, bound in chains and enclosed in iron cages, were many captives taken from the raids of the last torturous years, including Wilderfrant's queen Emilorthan, whom he had longed to see again before the end. But he did not pray for this manner. Flat on his face, with blood dripping from his mouth and his veins bubbling, Wilderfrant smiled at his queen. And then Haegos, now with the Crown of Ithyendor fitted firm on his head, stabbed King Wilderfrant VII through the spine.

On Trilsenya and Medwyn

If there was any triumph to be had in the year 2332 then, it did not come from the Angelons. But they were not the only nation still fighting the long struggle against Haegos; so too were the Lycemeans, led by the beautiful King Trilsenya, now missing her face.

If the reader is now beckoning back to prior pages, let it be assured that this is a new development, for the fate of Trilsenya was brushed over in the previous chapter to allow a straight narrative following the blue prince Erfrant. But now we take a short leap back to that evil night of Lay Pork, to briefly summarize the exploits of Trilsenya upon that night.

She had led a charge to relieve the overwhelmed Angelon forces, along with her fellow commander and friend Wheatlank the Unshaven. When the lights went out and perpetual darkness took hold, Trilsenya and Wheatlank nonetheless forged forward, knowing that if they held their horses on a straight course, they would eventually collide with the Tower of Haegos. This they did, and the Lycemean riders behind helped to breach the gates.

The interior was dimly lit, though it seemed as broad daylight to those who had spent an hour in the endless black. Their eyes adjusted, and quickly the Lycemeans realized that this entrance chamber was designed as a trap. There was nowhere for them to go; all of the stairwells radiating from this courtyard were blocked by thick bars. Trilsenya looked up, and saw a host of archers standing atop a balcony, with bows pointed down at the lot of them.

"We've come only for the captives. Release your prisoners and we leave in peace, never to return," bartered the fair queen. In response, thrown down to them from the balcony was the fresh corpse of perhaps the mostly highly valued of Haegos' prisoners: Himgo the Tall, younger brother of Prince Erfrant, and heir to the throne of Angelon should Erfrant meet an untimely death. "You've made a blunder of judgement," scowled Trilsenya as she looked up at the archers, after giving the body of Himgo a parting caress.

"I believe the blunder belongs to you, most of all," spoke a familiar voice from above. Out from shadow strode Peril of Enceloth, finely clothed in royal purple. He began to speak at length to all in that doomed courtyard, of his love for Trilsenya and how her rejection led him to that place—

Wheatlank shot him with an arrow— one attached to a string — and as the arrow stuck into Peril's shoulder, Wheatlank yanked, pulling him over his safety ledge and down into the courtyard. Perhaps this arrow was a mistake, for now there was no hope of bargain. Now there was only chaos, and death. Volleys of arrows were fired in all directions. Trilsenya lifted up Peril and held his neck at the point of a dagger, calling for a swift end to the violence.

But the men above cared not for Peril, and very much wanted to see the Lycemeans burn, and so they pulled a rope. The rope triggered the release of a burning oil from above, which splashed down upon the Lycemeans like a rain of wrath. Here, seeing her opportunity quickly failing, Trilsenya plunged her dagger into the eye of Peril. In all of recorded history, this is the singular moment when the House of Lycema ever committed an act of violence towards the House of Enceloth, and many say it was well deserved.

But then did the rains of burning oil return, for twelve more rounds, and by the end of it, nearly all the Lycemeans lay dead in a pile of melted flesh. Trilsenya, being king, was saved from death by her peoples, who sheltered her from the rains of wrath. She crouched down on the body of one already dead while other sheltering soldiers sat atop her, but even then, oil seeped through the cracks and she was badly burned like all the rest. After the shelterers too had perished, it was the deeds of Wheatlank that would save the Lycemean monarch. For Wheatlank the Unshaven climbed the stone wall, up to the courtyard's balcony, and there devoured her enemies with unshaven fury.

After scouring the halls of the tower, the only unguarded exit was found to be a sewage tunnel with a sharp drop. Trilsenya failed to catch herself in this sharp drop, and found herself fallen into a deep puddle of molten oil, the same which had been collected and weaponized above. This heinous flow of the enemy dissolved both of Trilsenya's, and would by the end of the night take her nose and ears as well. In this way, the lovely King Trilsenya came to be faceless.

We return to 2332 then, when a veiled Trilsenya stood by the shore of the sea, on the beach at Medwyn. Like the city of Frawlin in Angelon, this town of Medwyn had become the last defense for the realm of Lycema, which had once spread far to the east. Trilsenya chose to be optimistic about the situation, however, and said that at least they had been able to hold the city on the tip of the sea.

For she loved the sea. And now that she was without sight, hearing the crashing waves of the water turned into a routine of great importance for her. Wheatlank remained always at her side, feeling in some ways responsible for Trilsenya's injuries. But the King of Lycema kept her resilience, and even joked that she had given a blessing in losing her sight, for now she never again had to look upon the shit-lands that had so been made into shit by the defecational deeds of Haegos.

"You are right about that," nodded Wheatlank, "And I am nodding right now. For all the lands have turned to feces. But while we have lived these past nine years in a relative harmony here at Medwyn, news comes now that Haegos will attempt to shit on us even here. For the old Young King Wilderfrant is now dead— bested in sole combat with Haegos at Ansila Siroth, and so awoke his thirst for blood. He will now end his war, by taking all cities that defy him, and surely Medwyn shall be first upon that list."

"Then we must fight shit with urine," spoke Trilsenya, stoically. What the famous king of Lycema meant by this, none have been able to say for certain. But it is recorded in all chronicles regarding the Battle of Medwyn, and therefore it must be of some importance.

To briefly relate the battle, one could say that the defenses of Medwyn planted themselves on the beach with the sea at their backs, and simply did not move. The forces of Haegos were led this time by Shiron, and he laughed when he saw the strategy of Trilsenya and Wheatlank. "They are not ten meters from the sea!" He laughed to the disgusting freaks in his army. "We will drive them forward with ease and the water will do our bidding for us— they will be drowned within minutes!" And so, cumming with overconfidence to the highest degree, Shiron marched forward on the beach.

But the Lycemeans fought beyond the word fiercely, for they were fighting for their home, and all the homes before it, so that this— their last home— would not be taken in the same manner. While some did remain planted firmly through the whole of the fight, others were drawn back into the sea— but this was no deathly matter for them, who had all been swimming habitually for the last generation.

It was Shiron's forces who succumbed to the water, falling in the waves as if they were flames. For the simple truth was that the armies of Haegos had never found much use in the teachings of fish, and so none in his army could swim. And so they naturally assumed the same to be true of their opponents, who— as previously stated— were actually skillful when wet. In truth then, the Sea of Cathuma can be called just a much a victor of Medwyn as can be Trilsenya and Wheatlank.

But the true victory came later that day, as Trilsenya and Wheatlank led their famous charge, with a line of horsemen behind, chasing the final ranks of Shiron from the beach and off into the setting sun in the east. Shiron himself was captured, and to him a particularly cruel fate was handed. For his body was slowly dismembered upon the beach, in holding with an ancient Nephinarthin tradition, from the tips of the extremities to the core. When all limbs and extraneous organs had been severed and chopped into six hundred pieces, these were set around Shiron in a circle, and all lit ablaze. Then the living stump of the limbless man was tossed into the sea, to be helplessly drowned in the shallows.

On Wilfrant the Stone King

The free pockets of civilization rejoiced to hear of the victory at Medwyn, for news still found a way of spreading in those days, even through dense evil lands. So fearful of the victorious Lycemeans were the Vexen that they even conceded much of their territory to the northwest of Medwyn, so that Trilsenya could hold command over the great road that led from her city to Frawlin. In this way, she came to visit her distant relation, the new king of Angelon, Wilderfrant IX. This boy king was only aged 21 years, and had taken to be called Wilfrant, to avoid confusion with his predecessors.

Trilsenya counseled young Wilfrant, and spoke long of her great victory at Medwyn. Wilfrant, too, would come to have a great victory in coming days if he heeded her words, she said. But Wilfrant, like his father Erfrant, had not caught the love of war that had been present in prior men of his line. In fact, he was even less disposed to war than his father. Instead of at least recognizing his duty and giving it a go, Wilfrant simply decided to leave his country (which, to be fair, was currently the size of one city).

How this came to be is laid chiefly upon the legs of one man: a woman named Tira, whom Wilfrant had met while out riding in the desolation of the charred woods outside Arthconendin. There he stumbled upon a blackened shack, with all inside burned and very little replaced. For Tira had been turned orphan nine years ago, while still a child, when the raging Vexen armies swept up into the north following the massacre at Lay Pork.

"I hear epic tales of orphan girls becoming great warriors," spoke Tira to Wilfrant in her crumbling abode. "Like when Witlonk Firespear was slain and his daughter rose up in his place, to surpass even her famous father in glory. But losing my own parents did not bring me such a desire for vengeance. I have no thirst for the blood of any, not even those who have taken everything from me. Rather I wish only to live in a world where we can do without such things. I wish for a world where there are no swords." And so she grabbed Wilfrant's hands, and turned him into a full and complete pacifist.

Now it is fine and perhaps even noble to be a pacifist; there is no argument there. The argument arrives, however, when the pacifist in question happens to be the lord of a realm, in the midst of an ongoing struggle, whose people depend on him for their safety and preservation. Wilfrant did not consider the position of his people or the nature of their enemies for that matter, and away he fled, with Tira in his arms and Tira in his cheeks.

In his stead he left a stone likeness, not the craft of mediocs or of recreational carvers, but a stunning statue of marble stone which even appeared to be human. The face was both sad and wise, with a complexity of additional emotions melted into the subtleties of the face. One passing by in dim light could easily be excused for mistaking this magnificent carving for the king himself. And so it was not with a heavy heart that Wilfrant abandoned his folk, for in this stone likeness he believed the Angelons would have a better ruler than he himself would have proven.

At first, the rule of the Stone King proved to be remarkably and unbelievably effective. For the nobles would stand before it and ask questions, seeking advice and counsel on their actions, and the Stone King would either life a hand for an affirmative, lower a hand for a negative, and flick fingers to present a number. In this way, the nobles of Angelon decided their course in raids and sieges, and how many men to muster in each. For three years this met with surprisingly grand results, and they gained back much of their former territory. Men began to praise the Stone King as a god, for their fortunes had never run higher in recent memory.

Word of this came to Pendala, where Wilfrant and Tira were enjoying their self-imposed exile. They lived in a charming cottage of bright color along a small stretch of white sand, with crystal blue water sprawling in front of them. Vibrant palms lined the walk to their home, and exotic birds and bushes abounded in all directions. In every way, this was the lush and hospitable land that the Angelons dreamed of but would never know, for the armies of Haegos prevented any kind of mass migration outwards from their capital at Frawlin. But Wilfrant and Tira had been able to escape their homelands undetected, with stealth and cunning, and they laughed about it now.

For the first handful of years, Wilfrant kept to his walls, for fear that any neighbors might discover his true identity as King Wilderfrant IX, the deserter of that miserable land to the south. But as the years lagged on, and Tira grew from a pretty enough lady into a surprisingly fox-like man, Wilfrant began to feel the urge to show her off. She would sit in their seaside cottage in small shirts, for the weather always encouraged sweat, and her shoulders would become a golden brown, and Wilfrant could not resist. He found his pleasure to be amply doubled when he boasted to others about the satisfaction he felt deep in his wife. And this would prove to be his undoing, but first we must speak of DANE.

DANE was the child of Himgo the Tall, as well as Wilfrant's older cousin. He, like the rest of the Angelon nobility, stood before the Stone King everyday for quite a few years. However, unlike much of the nobility, DANE found it all to be quite ridiculous. He knew there was nothing divine about the Stone King, and that it had simply been a ruse to placate the people whilst his peace-loving cousin skipped off with his bride to some distant pasture. But still DANE rode off with his men, to perform raids and sieges on the enemy. He predicted that one day the Stone King would fail them, and this proved true.

In 2336 the Stone King had given the signals to mount a siege upon Haegos' castle in Hestleren. DANE happened to be sick at the time of this, and so he did not go. This was lucky for both him and for history, for every man who partook in that siege was eaten by wolves. The fact that DANE— who always resented the Stone King and its tellings— just happened to be sick and avoided the fate of his comrades, proved to be too much of a coincidence for the Angelon elders to handle. So they exiled DANE out of suspicion. And thus DANE came to walk the earth, fending off against Vexen and Desiroth, and often times mixing with them and learning their ways.

Yet DANE never stopped looking for a way back into the hearts of the Angelons. In 2341, he devised that the best way to return home would be to bring back the most noblest of offerings: the key to the city of Angelon Othim. Still was this capital of old held in a chokehold, with the Archangel of Cathuma sitting atop his throne on a tall spire. But always was there a master key to unlock all the many gates located on all sides of the city, and if this key would happen to fall back into the hands of the Angelons they might retake the city through sneaking and trickery. Or so thought DANE.

So DANE imbedded himself into a camp of Vexen, finding them truly not to be all that bad, and thus found access into that glorious haven of Angelon Othim. Once within the city gates, DANE sped to the old King's Hall, the roof of which had been torn off long ago and the pillars leveled. Green vines now twisted their way through all the cracked stone. But still DANE remembered the maps and plans he had studied as a child, and he ran forward in the dead of night. There, beside the great vault which once housed the Crown of Ithyendor, was the Key to the City, just lying there. Could it really be so simple to just lift the key and head off? Yes. That part would be just so simple. But not ten counts later, DANE found himself under the fiery pursuit of Desiroth guards.

DANE fled out of Angelon Othim and directly to the marshlands of the Andiloth, where he believed he would fare well in losing his chasers. But as he began running across the wobbling bridges that moved this way and that across the swampy waters, the son of Himgo fell flat upon his stomach. And quickly felt around for the key, finding it lost. Already. And as a mob of swordsmen came crashing onto the unstable bridge in the dark, DANE realized that he had absolutely no chance of recovering it. And so he simply leapt into the reeds, and endured a swampy night, catching rest upon muck and log.

He returned to Frawlin a dirty man, but a dirty man with knowledge. He spoke at length about all he witnessed at Angelon Othim, and that it was not so heavily guarded as all had assumed. And he emphasized to no end how he had indeed recovered the Key to the City before finding it lost in the marshlands.

The nobles, all of them aged twenty years in the last five, mulled over their options and told DANE that they must first consult the Stone King. To this, DANE nodded and stepped in ahead of them, knocking the Stone King to the ground and breaking its arms off. The elder nobles gasped, and an all-out war ensued that made the war with Haegos appear petty. But order was restored by the night, mainly on account of King Trilsenya of Lycema being summoned.

She had always admired DANE, and saw in him a great future — though not in a literal sense, since both of her eyes had been put out on the night of Lay Pork. But she held a firm voice over the nobles, and so it was decided that a full-scale attack be sent to reclaim Angelon Othim. To ensure that the Plain of Sashara to the north of the city was truly clear of opposition, DANE was sent forth first with a team of the fastest riders, and they swept along eastward, slaying all the stray Desiroth they found in their path.

The greater forces then marched east from Frawlin alongside the Andiloth, until they found themselves positioned directly across from their old city— that which had been founded by Francil, first monarch of their nation. What ensued was poised to be the retribution for Lay Pork, eighteen years on, with the aging disgruntleds and newly mustered generation of Angelons all fighting side by side at the gates of their enemy.

From their position across the river, the Angelons fired great catapults and trebuchets of burning stone and heavied lance. Their presumption of drawing out the armies of Haegos from the city into open battle in the daylight, however, fell short on their hopes. Had the opponent come to the river and drifted across, the Angelons might have held some resistance, picking off the barges and once again using the enemy's dread fear of water against them. Haegos, however, anticipated this, and the legions were not set out til nightfall.

The Angelons were here not so utterly unprepared for dark as they had been upon Lay Pork. With great torches they lit the night, and burned sprawling pits with mountainous flame so that they would see their enemy full. Swift and out of darkness did the dwindling Desiroth leap onto the battlefield, but the well-rested soldiers of Frawlin had their sharpness perked, and by the light of their fires would clamp swords into the bellies of their foe as they descended upon them. In this way, the Battle of Sashara proved to be truly a fight, instead of simply a massacre.

Yet do not grow hopeful, dear and pleasant reader, for the Plains of Sashara did not hold victory in store for the peoples of Wilderfrant. As the night dragged on into its center, when stars shone at their brightest, the Desiroth began to encircle their adversaries. Dark was the night even with the assistance of flame, and the high commands did not come from a place of far sight. In fact, they came from a place of no sight, for King Trilsenya was still without eyes, and served more as a symbolic inspiration for the troops. Wheatlank the Unshaven stood by close at hand, forever protecting the Lycemean king, and horning out the better of the commands. Yet even she could not begin to realize that their enemies were closing in on all sides.

The battle snaked left and right, weaving along the river and about the plain in a haphazard manner, with the only strategy of the Angelons being to slaughter whatever they found at the tip of their swords. Many of the men fighting on the fringes of the field then found escape that night, but the forces of Haegos tightened in upon the rest, forming seven circles of densely packed legions with nowhere to go, lest they cut their way through Desiroth layers so thick that a hand could not be plunged into it farther than an arm's length. With these seven circles formed, the enemy from its stronghold in Angelon Othim sent out a decisive blow that would end the battle most definitely.

All at once, seven massive boulders of flame were propelled from craft of high aim, and they soared across starlit sky from the city over the Andiloth. The trapped soldiers looked up, all of them seeing this final vision of dazzling glory rushing towards them. The boulders of flame struck their marks, each one, and crushed the remaining armies of Frawlin in one swift moment. Thus ended a hopeful night of promise, fated to join the list of terrible defeats found all along the dripping lips of Haegos.

Word of the crushing blows of Sashara wound its way to Pendala. And deserter King Wilfrant said to his wife Tira that it was a great relief not to have been there. For truly, Wilfrant had fled his own people fearing a great day of reckoning that might burn akin to the memory of heinous Lay Pork, and that night had come. While it had come, he was enjoying the flesh of his lady upon a beach of pure white sand, with gentle night wind tickling him to the sound of the ocean's living waves.

Wilfrant enjoyed night such as these, especially knowing the alternative, but still he had grown fatigued of this peaceful existence, and sought a hint of stimulation in this ninth year of his exile. He began to frequent the seaside shores of Pendala, with its great public fountains and pools. On the palm-filled paths he would engage the brown-skinned men of that land and speak plainly to the fairness of his bride. The boastful presence of one so strange to their customs brought the Pendalese to words, and these words sailed the web current that led ever back to Haegos and Melizar. It was to the farthest north, then, that they would seek to find their lost king.

They sent out Khahir, a man who had recently been proclaimed the new Duke of Mangiloth, first to hold that office since Thaegoce. For the politics of that realm were shifted when Jasper brought the whole of Dikenia under the spell of Melizar, and thus relinquished his hold over Mangiloth. Whereas under the rule of Jasper Mangiloth had been subservient to Dikenia, now Dikenia was brought into utter slavery under the vast hand of Mangiloth. And their Grand Duke Khahir— appointed for his cunning and sadness— was the great driver of the slaves, with a belt lined of whips, and an assortment of vile hooks trailing off his sleeves.

Khahir arrived in Pendala without betraying his identity, and towards the end of the year found himself upon the doorstep of Wilfrant and Tira. Posing as one who would pay the price of his fourteen wives for one night with Tira, Khahir struck a deal with Wilfrant. But upon the day of payment, it was fourteen pale white Dikenian slave girls that were brought up the beach to Wilfrant's home. Seeing this, the king in exile would have quickly surmised the identity of Khahir as Mangiloth's infamous new duke, and would have bolted for the hills. But not a moment after it dawned on him, the back doors of his cottage were cut down with axe and the windows shattered through by Desiroth tongue. It is not known what became of Tira on this day, though one can assume that her tale did not end in joyous affair.

Wilderfrant IX was bound and carried off down narrow wooded path, down the slopes towards the camp of Khahir, now first commander to dreaded Haegos. Here the Stone King was flayed alive, so that all the things under his flesh were therefore seen by all who were near, with nauseating hues of purple and pink that made one gasp with a horrid sense of exposure. They took him before Haegos, and here Wilfrant pleaded for his life to be spared, however secretly hoping that his life would be taken instantly then and there, for he had no desire to live a second more in the world without skin, a world which had become more painful than the cruelest of horrid eyelids.

But Haegos was incapable of mercy, and could see through this all too predictable trick. He granted to Wilfrant that his life would indeed be spared, and bade the Stone King to live out another two weeks— force fed and watered— with no blankets nor even flesh to keep him warm. Eventually though, blankets were an absolute necessity in prolonging the miserable life of this de-throned monarch, for he had taken ill just days after his capture. With no skin to ward of the dirty airs, infections of all kinds began to set in rather quickly, and the guards of Wilfrant's cage— who themselves were accustomed to the most inhumane of prison conditions— found the Stone King's afflictions to be nothing short of ghastly.

With shivers to no end, mixed with an eternal rasp of the throat and involuntary wheezing, discoloration and throbbing of the muscles and arteries, it was clear that this royal captive would not live out the time it would take to carry him back to Angelon Othim. So attentive care was granted for the sake of Haegos' grand design, along with medicinal herbs and fluid. The journey down to Angelon Othim commenced, and by the time they drew near to the overrun city, Wilfrant's skin had begun to grow back, and was already more or less half that of a normal unflayed man. So Khahir's men flayed him anew.

Freshly de-skinned, Wilderfrant IX emerged out of his dark carriage for the first time since his capture, into the central courtyard of Angelon Othim. There, he was seen by the entire population of the city, for Haegos had commanded his garrison to round up every soul within a hundred miles and ensure they all saw the doom of those who desired to be free. They were slaves now, all the lot of them, and those who did not serve Haegos would share in the same doom as their former king.

The ramparts were stacked high, the roofs overflowing— for the courtyard of Angelon Othim was never meant to accommodate a crowd the size of thousands. Fifty wermen and eighty women died that day from the pushings of crowd alone, either falling off balconies or by being trampled by fellow spectators. But in that crowd was one who would not be so easily silenced: the cousin of the king, son of Himgo the Tall— younger son of Wilderfrant VII— who we all know to be DANE. And as DANE stood close to the stage on that smoky day in Angelon Othim, he held hidden a clenched fist as he watched the unraveling fate of his younger cousin.

For Wilderfrant IX, beheld by all his peoples as a skinless wretch, was then drenched in boiled water, dumped on him from a tub which Khahir's men held overhead. The Stone King lie there then, on the brink of imminent death, his breaths becoming quick and then very slow. To end the life of his adversary and send a burning message of finality, Haegos covered the royal body in a thick black tar.

He then held Wilderfrant IX by the neck, thrusting it forward and demanding the people to cry out horrid curses against. Out of fear and following the lead of the many Ansilian officers standing within them, the citizens of Angelon Othim roared out obscenities and murderous hate at the tarred corpse of the skinless king.

It is said the only man who abstained from this monstrosity was DANE.

On DANE and His Deeds

You may think that this horrendous double flaying, boiling and tarring of the Stone King Wilderfrant IX may suffice to serve as the defining moment of cruelty from all the wars of Haegos. In truth, many argue this public execution to surpass even the misery of Lay Pork, for here all the cruelty was put to one werman. It may well be the peak of cruelty, but devastation did not there end. As resistance once again began to brew in the weeks following the royal execution, the armies of Haegos snapped in anger under the realization that no single thing could put them into submission, no matter how heinous. And so hostilities recommenced, and the Angelons were driven out to the farthest reaches.

Meanwhile, DANE harbored a fury over his cousin's execution, and put forth a hasty action— the type of which he would become known for. Only fourteen people attended his coronation in the fecal chambers of Frawlin, and the majority of these were elder women who thought they had stumbled into bird songs of old. For the peoples of Frawlin saw no use in the crowning of a new king; surely he would come to be flayed and oiled and tarred just as the last.

DANE had a restless night. Instead of simply waiting til the dawn and allowing his times of sleep to be ruined, he decided to set out immediately on a fool's quest. He and a small group of select companions made for Enthin Croth, a wide fort on the southern marshes of Lycema, just north of the Hollow Rounds. Of course this was Lycema no longer, for valiant as faceless Trilsenya was, she had long lost all her territory save the Medwyn Road.

Too long, argued DANE, had the enemy mustered darkness as their ally and used it against them. On this night, he spoke of a surprise attack, wherein he and his men would rush in stealthily with the ailments of true surprise. And so the company left their horses on the ridge and balled on stealthily to the burned out fort of Enthin Croth. There, they snuck around crumbling stone and brick walls, towards the source of whispering devilry.

There in the central courtyard, they saw both Haegos and his prized commander, Khahir. It was perhaps too magnificent a chance to be an honest dance. But an honest dance it was, and had the archers of DANE prevailed in shooting Khahir through the neck, the war might have ended there. But rather, DANE succumbed to a mortal hastiness and charged Haegos with a furious wrath. He battered the silent iron demon to the ground, subduing his stench with strike upon strike, and there he may have succeeded in killing him if not for the intervention of Khahir— who unleashed a heinous cross between wolf and bear, to kill all of them well. All were slain except DANE, who was released after much taunting, for Khahir spoke of his desire to execute only kings, and DANE now lorded over none. Go back to his kingdom, he was told, if indeed he could find it. For as of late, there was no kingdom to return to.

Frawlin was razed. The town that had served as the Angelon capital for the last forty years, and the only Angelon town at all for the last twenty, was abruptly smeared off the map. The city of Angelon Othim— though not held by the Angelons since 2291— was destroyed by earthquake just to spite the once proud peoples. This was brought about by the Archangel of Cathuma, now wearing the Crown of Ithyendor upon his own otherworldly head, and with its power bringing about the city's total destruction. This once great settlement of civilization would remain in ruins for thousands of years, even down into my own time.

The Angelons then, with no cities or land to lay claim to, held a brief ceremony dissolving their nation, as they were chased into the west by bloody blade. The nation had lasted 457 years, seemingly falling just 43 years short of the old Prophecy of the Manes. To the great peaks of the Sashites the people fled, for no other place would ensure their survival. Here then, communities of thousands were broken into tight units, fending for only their closest relation and reverting back into a tribal mind, among the beasts of the hills.

For six years this existence of hunger and scarcity reigned supreme among all who had been beaten by Haegos. But all the while, DANE would not forget the visions of Prince Erfrant, nor the sight of cousin Wilfrant succumbing to an ultimate evil. In the high peaks of the Northward Sashites he rallied what folks could understand his tongue. Reluctant were all to take back battle to an enemy so undefeatable— indeed their only triumphs had been in 2279 and 2332, only under special circumstance— but DANE was a valiant man with a voice that spoke of honor and sacrifice, freedom and dignity, courage and strength, and an eventual victory. So the folk rallied to him.

2247 was the year of their last great defeat. A defeat so awful that it paled Lay Pork in comparison. For Khahir had purposely let the location of Ansila Siroth slip to his outer forces, who raided the Sashites where the Angelons now hid. DANE slit the throat of on Ansilian, about to slit another when he was offered this great piece of knowledge. DANE then kept this Ansilian alive, to serve as guide so that he himself might behold the fabled city deep within jagged black stone, and then overthrow it. His mountain men were assembled, and this desperate raid rode forth, with not an ounce of hope in any of them.

Perhaps it was this lack of faith that proved their undoing. Or perhaps it was simply that they were an army of a hundred going into the capital of their enemy, a million strong. Whatever the reason, they were slaughtered as always. DANE's guide led them into Ansila Siroth true enough, and there in the black valley they beheld a stationary army of 5600. Though as they weaved their way down, they came to realize that this army of 5600 was not moving at all, for they were dead in their entirety. They were the doomed casualties of war from generations passed, brought here to Ansila Siroth to stand erect and plastered into place, to serve as a symbol of Haegosian might, that all who were once his enemies would eventually stand before his tower in an upright death.

Warily did the hundred men of DANE wade through this army of the dead erect, feeling uneasy to see the faces of those taken fifty years back so well preserved through a transparent goop of an orange hue. "Disturbing, is it not?" Were the last words of one, who then quickly found out that not all in this crowd were dead. For interlaced with these thousands of these soul-departed bodies were just as many Ansilian forces: Desiroth, Vexen, and Dikenian, all ideally stacked to lash upon DANE's men in utter surprise. DANE knew not where to look. All around where the armored suits of those dead, but among these his men were flown away in the space of a fractional moment. Leaping through the array of preserved casualties the Ansilians took them, and placed them all in a deep pit, where quickly the hundred of them piled to the top.

Here, the men thrown in first might be considered lucky. For they were most likely crushed instantly, as their fellow soldiers came falling upon them from great height. Those in the middle of the pile succumbed to suffocation. But those thrown in last, on top of the pit, were doused in a flood of flammable liquid, and then set ablaze. Once again DANE was apprehended, and placed in an ideal position just over this pit, to watch his brave forces die in mangled agony. Here then, the enemy made their fatal decision for a second time, and allowed DANE to cower back to his castrated kingdom unscathed. The torment of the mind that they had inflicted upon him would be far crueler than allowing him to die. And so DANE fled out of Ansila Siroth, his purpose there completely unfulfilled.

He shivered as he glanced back upon the narrow stone passage, looking down upon a slithering rush of flame, that which had extinguished the last faith of a truly courageous lot. With them they had brought a last desperate strike into a land without mercy, and with their passing perished all hope, and all the lands were without shelter.

For now to all the world it was proved that the dread armies of Haegos were truly unstoppable.

56

Flowery Epilogue

But time would come to show that they were not. For the end of war did come, three years after, in the glorious turn of 2350. DANE won the day, and the armies of Haegos were wiped from Overlind. Yet one great victory cannot take back nor amend for 75 years of horror. The memories of those heinous days would remain in the hearts of good men for time immemorial, and so have passed to me. The Battle of Gizelia— where DANE at last saved the kingdom— is well documented to the tune of a hundred pages, and so would be utterly daunting to speak of here. Let it suffice to say that things all worked themselves out. Or that perhaps great evil will always find its end by the very being of its own destructive nature. For I am grown tired in this pit, and shall relate no more.

5656565656565656565656565656565656565656565656565656565656

Made in the USA
Monee, IL
19 December 2019